Hers for the Summer

Jill Kemerer

D0172813

🍃 **LOVE INSPIRED**
INSPIRATIONAL ROMANCE

LOVE INSPIRED®
INSPIRATIONAL ROMANCE

ISBN-13: 978-1-335-48873-2

Hers for the Summer

Copyright © 2021 by Ripple Effect Press, LLC

Recycling programs
for this product may
not exist in your area.

This edition published by arrangement with Harlequin Books S.A.

For questions and comments about the quality of this book,
please contact us at CustomerService@Harlequin.com.

Love Inspired
22 Adelaide St. West, 40th Floor
Toronto, Ontario M5H 4E3, Canada
www.Harlequin.com

Printed in U.S.A.

He brought me forth also into a large place:
he delivered me, because he delighted in me.
—*2 Samuel* 22:20

To my sister, Sarah.
Writing this book brought back so many
good memories of growing up in the country,
riding bikes, playing with our dolls, arguing,
giggling and always having each other's backs.
I love you!

Chapter One

Maybe she wasn't meant to be a mommy. Maybe she was only meant to nurture other people's children.

Eden Page tucked her hands into the pockets of her winter coat as she strode toward Cattle Drive Coffee. The air was clear and cold, typical for Rendezvous, Wyoming, in mid-April. It had been another long, never-ending winter. Signs of spring were all around, though. Green shoots of flower bulbs poked out in front of the bank across the street, and a few of the trees had loosened their grips on the tight buds capping off their branches. For the first time since her sister died, Eden wondered if spring was on its way in her own life, too.

Mia had been gone for almost five years. Since then Eden had been drifting along, babysitting full-time for friends and waiting and hoping for Mr. Right to show up. Unfortunately, Mr. Wrong hadn't even knocked on her door at this point.

For as long as Eden could remember, she'd wanted to get married, have children and live in Rendezvous, preferably on a ranch. She didn't regret quitting college to be here for Mia's final months, and she was thankful she'd been able to babysit her nephew, Noah, until Mason Fanning, Mia's husband, got remarried last year. Eden still spent a lot of time with the five-year-old boy.

Rounding the corner, she picked up her pace. It was time to accept reality. While only twenty-six, she might never get married or have children. The guys around here weren't interested in her and never had been. If she didn't take charge of her life soon, another five years would pass by with little to show for them, either.

The faded maroon awning above the coffee shop entrance came into view. Maybe she could finish her degree in early childhood education and get a job teaching preschool. Or expand her babysitting services.

"Howdy, Eden." Mr. Jenkins, her favorite usher from church, tipped his cowboy hat to her as he walked his two black Labs. He got around well for a man his age. "Think it'll snow tonight?"

"I hope not. I'm ready for warmer weather." She gave him a smile and petted the dogs. Their tongues lolled as they lifted pet-me eyes to her. Chuckling, she scratched behind their ears.

"At least it's Friday, right?" His brown eyes twinkled. "You have big plans?"

She did not have big plans. She didn't have *any* plans.

"I'm keeping it low-key." She gave the dogs' ears a final scratch. "What about you?"

"There's a World War II documentary on I've been looking forward to." He tugged on the leashes, and the dogs moved forward. "Well, I won't keep you. See you Sunday."

"Enjoy yourself." She opened the door to the coffee shop. Her night sounded even less exciting than Mr. Jenkins's. At least he had a documentary to look forward to. She had nothing. Normally, she offered to babysit Noah so Mason and Brittany could have some couple time, but the three of them had other plans this evening.

The coffee shop was almost empty, and why wouldn't it be? Friday nights were for hanging out with friends, ordering pizza or going to Roscoe's for burgers—not for heavily caffeinated beverages.

The warmth of the room and hardwood floors drew her forward, and she ordered her favorite latte. While the teenager behind the counter prepared the drink, Eden turned to stare out the front windows. A young couple laughed as they strolled past arm in arm. Across the street, Eden could just make out Stu Miller helping Gretchen Sable out of his truck. Stu and Gretchen were in their seventies, and they'd managed to find love. Why couldn't she?

She couldn't even get a date. It was like she was invisible to men. Was it too much to ask for a little romance?

"Here you go." The girl handed her the cup and began wiping down the counter like her life depended on it. The shop didn't officially close for another hour. She probably had plans, too.

Back outside, Eden braced herself against the chill. Her apartment wasn't far. Last year she'd moved out of her parents' house into the apartment above Brittany Fanning's dance studio. Eden was glad Mason had married Brittany, although it was strange to think of him married to anyone other than her sister.

What was she going to do about her future? She loved babysitting, but it didn't offer benefits like paid vacations or retirement plans, and taking care of her best friend Gabby's eighteen-month-old daughter, Phoebe, a few days a week wasn't exactly paying the bills. After selling the family ranch last year, Eden's parents had blessed her with a lump sum of money. She kept her expenses low, but it was a relief to have the financial cushion now that Gabby no longer needed her to babysit Phoebe full-time.

Pale pink and lavender streaked the sky as the sun slid down the horizon. She wrapped both hands around the takeout cup and sipped it as she turned onto Third Street. The coffee warmed her insides, kicking her pulse up a notch. She barely glanced at the bungalow converted into a dentist office or the parking lot with dead grass poking out of the cracked blacktop. Up ahead, the dance studio and her apartment beckoned.

Her phone dinged. She pulled it out of her pocket.

Ryder.

Blech.

Of all the people she did *not* want to deal with tonight, Ryder Fanning topped the list. It was inconceivable that Mason could have an identical twin so unlike him. Where Mason was quiet and thought things through, Ryder lacked patience and didn't consider how his words or actions affected the people around him.

The man annoyed her.

She shoved the phone back in her pocket and took a long drink of the coffee.

Her stride lengthened as she neared the dance studio. She cut through the side parking lot, headed to the rear and climbed the stairs leading to her apartment. When she reached the top of the landing, she paused. As she stared at the door, a terrible loneliness crept in.

Everyone she knew and loved was moving on. Her closest friends were either married or engaged. Even her parents had embarked on a new life, traveling around the country in their RV. She wasn't sure she could spend another night alone flipping through the channels.

For a moment she wished something—anything—would happen to relieve the monotony of her life.

Her phone dinged again, and she unlocked the door and went inside. Did she even want to know why Ryder was texting her? It wasn't only his lack of filter she resented.

He was the one who'd bought the family ranch.

After Dad told her in January that Ryder Fanning was buying the only home she'd ever known, she'd driven to her special place outside town and cried until her tears froze. It had put the first deep crack in her hopes for the future. The life she'd always imagined truly had no chance of reviving at this point.

She'd thought she'd get married and spend Christmases in the old farmhouse, baking with her children, hanging out with her parents. But all those hopes died when Ryder bought the ranch.

Next week he was moving to Rendezvous from Los Angeles. For the past two months he'd been having the house remodeled. Her house. Hopefully, she'd never have to go inside. It would break her heart. She'd made a million memories there with Mia. They'd shared secrets, held grudges, played games.

Eden sighed, juggling the coffee as she took off her coat and kicked off her shoes. Her phone began to ring, and she glared at it until it stopped.

She had nothing to say to him.

When it started ringing again, she marched down the hall to the kitchen, gritting her teeth the entire way. Persistence was Ryder's middle name. He'd just keep bothering her until she answered. She might as well get it over with.

"What do you want?" she asked.

"Oh, hey, you answered." Ryder's low voice had the same effect on her as the warm latte. It heated her insides and jolted her pulse to life. Unlike with the latte, she didn't enjoy the sensation. "I've got something to ask you."

His phrasing implied a favor, and she didn't do favors for him. Eden adored Ryder's cute five-year-old identical twin girls, but she did not like their daddy. Not one bit.

"Eden?"

"I'm busy." A bold lie, even for her.

"I know. It's important, though, and I don't want to discuss it over the phone. I'm in Rendezvous."

"Sorry, I can't." *Won't* was more like it. And she wasn't sorry. Not at all.

"I'll only take a minute of your time."

A twinge of guilt hit her conscience, but she didn't respond.

"Will you give me one minute, Eden?"

A minute. Would she, the one who gladly gave hours and days and weeks to any of her friends at the drop of a hat, really deny Ryder sixty seconds?

It wouldn't kill her to hear what he had to say.

Then again, it might.

"Please?"

She'd never been able to turn down a heartfelt please. "Okay, but just for a minute. You can stop by my apartment." She looked around her place, grateful she was a neat freak.

"Good, because I'm right outside your door."

Of course he was.

Her heartbeat started doing the annoying hammering thing it tended to do in his vicinity. She was 99 percent sure it was her body's way of saying *don't even think about it*.

The man was good at getting his own way.

She, on the other hand, was used to letting other people have their way.

No wonder her danger signals were off the charts.

This was what she got for wishing something—anything—would happen instead of spending another Friday night flipping through the channels.

God surely had a sense of humor.

Eden padded to the door, girded her shoulders and took a deep breath. *Don't do anything stupid.* It was probably too late for that. Answering his call had been her first mistake. Opening this door was sure to be her next.

Ryder couldn't afford to make any more mistakes with his life. That was why he had to convince Eden to babysit the girls.

Starting over as a cattle rancher in the same town as his identical twin was the best decision he'd made in years. He'd have community, friends and the slower lifestyle he craved, not to mention he'd be able to raise Harper and Ivy out in the country far from Los Angeles.

It had been a dream come true to buy the large ranch from Eden's parents. His brother, Mason, was familiar with the property since he'd been married to Eden's sister before she died, and Ryder appreciated the fact Mason had urged him to purchase it. The renovations to the large farmhouse were almost complete. Ryder and his daughters were set to move to Rendezvous one week from tomorrow.

The life he wanted was within his grasp. And it was funny, but he hadn't even known he wanted it until recently.

He knocked on Eden's door. His nerves jittered as he tried to figure out how he could get her to agree to help him. He'd have to wing it. This conversation would be easier if she liked him. But she didn't. Not by a long shot.

He'd made a bad first, second, third and fourth impression on Eden. Had he ever made a good one?

Probably not, and it didn't matter. This was about his girls. They needed someone they could trust, who would love them and help them transition from a somewhat chaotic life in LA to a slower routine in Wyoming. And he needed to rest easy knowing Harper and Ivy were being well taken care of while he learned the ins and outs of raising cattle.

He knocked again.

His career as a CPA and financial planner for Hollywood bigwigs along with the divorce settlement from his ex-wife, actress Lily Haviland, had made him wealthy enough to buy the prime Wyoming property. And since he'd spent the first twelve years of his life on a sheep ranch, he wasn't a complete novice at ranching. But cattle? He didn't have much experience with those. Mason had been giving him tips every weekend that Ryder could make it back here, but he still had a lot to learn.

"Eden, it's me." He got the impression she was standing on the other side of the door. He could practically hear her breathing. Maybe that was wishful thinking. She was probably shimmying out a side window to escape.

The door opened, and he stared into the prettiest brown eyes he'd ever seen. A surge of warmth filled his gut. Every time he saw Eden, it was the same thing—he'd take one look at her, feel all warm and gooey inside and say something stupid. The woman had no idea how she affected him, and he wanted to keep it that way.

He wasn't getting entangled in a romance again. Look at how easily he'd been fooled by Lily. He'd believed every word that came out of his ex-wife's mouth, and they'd all turned out to be lies. The worst part about it was he didn't think Lily even intended to deceive him.

It came as naturally to her as slipping into the roles she played on television and the big screen.

The pain of being discarded by her still cut deep.

"Thanks for letting me come up." His voice was scratchy, although he'd downed a bottle of water on the way over.

Eden wasn't quite five and a half feet tall, and her body was slender, graceful. Dark brown hair fell in a silky curtain over her shoulders. Her delicate eyebrows arched just so under a high forehead. She wore slim-fitting black pants and a burgundy sweater hinting at curves underneath. She didn't crack a smile, but then, she was serious by nature.

Maybe that was what he found attractive. Her reserved personality. He'd never seen her flirt with any guys. She was generous to a fault with everyone—well, everyone except him.

"Come in." She pivoted and walked down the hallway. After closing the door, he followed her. He'd never been inside her apartment before.

"Nice place." He shrugged his arms out of his jacket and slung it over a bar stool near the counter. "The outside doesn't do it justice."

"It's been remodeled. Brittany let me help pick out everything." Eden sat on a chair in the living area and tucked one leg under her body.

The apartment was full of Eden touches. Cubbies and shelves brimming with children's books and toys lined the back wall of the dining area, and a colorful rug housed a pretend kitchen, doll crib and other assorted play items. The living room was all adult. Framed photos of Eden's parents and friends were placed on bookshelves along with novels, candles and photographs of nature.

"Did you take those?" He pointed to a collage of photos depicting the same view of nearby Silver Rocks River in spring, summer, fall and winter.

"Yes." She hugged one knee to her chest.

"They're great. I like how you captured it in all four seasons." When she didn't reply, he gestured to the gray couch. "Mind if I sit down?"

"Go ahead." She licked her lips and stared as if she wasn't quite sure what to do with him.

"The move is all set for next Saturday." Was that a flicker of anger in her eyes? Why would she be mad? "What? What was that look for?"

"Nothing."

"I know I'm not your favorite person, but do you have a problem with me moving here?"

"No." No emotion came through. "I don't love the fact you bought my parents' ranch."

"Oh." It had been on the market for a year. Her father had seemed relieved to sell it to him. He hadn't realized Eden wasn't in favor of the sale. "Why not?"

He regretted asking as soon as the words were out of his mouth. He braced himself for the truth. She probably thought he wasn't qualified to raise cattle and was assuming he'd fail at it.

He couldn't fail at it. He needed this change—needed to belong here.

"It's my childhood home."

"And?" His muscles unlocked. At least she hadn't accused him of incompetence.

"And I didn't want them to sell it." Her voice trailed off at the end, and she directed her gaze to the wall.

"Did you not want them to sell it to me?" he asked. "Or did you not want them to sell it at all?"

"At all."

Okay, he could work with that. As long as it wasn't him personally she objected to.

"Why are you here, Ryder? I know it's not to ask my blessing about you moving to my ranch."

Her ranch. His lips twitched. There had been a time in his life when bluntness would have put him on the defensive, but after everything Lily had put him through, he found bluntness—Eden's especially—refreshing.

"I need you to babysit the girls through the summer. This fall they'll be in kindergarten all day, but in the meantime, they need someone like you to help them adjust to their new life here."

A wistful smile brightened her face for a moment, but it disappeared behind a frown. "Chandra Davis runs a good day care program in town. Talk to her."

"I already did, and she's booked. She can't take the girls."

"Then find someone else."

"I've tried." He kept his tone gentle as frustration started to build. "Martha McNally has agreed to come to the ranch early every day so I can do my morning chores. She'll get the girls dressed and fed, then drive them here, so you wouldn't have to do anything but open your door for them at eight in the morning."

"Maybe Martha would watch them all day." She wouldn't meet his eyes. Annoyance flared up, catching him off guard.

"Look, Eden, I know I'm not your favorite person. When we first met, you were right to call me out for arguing with Lily on the phone in front of the girls."

"Your relationship with your ex-wife is none of my business. If the girls hadn't been completely crushed at the time, I wouldn't have mentioned it at all. It was ages ago. I'm over it."

Then why did she avoid him whenever he was in town? It was on the tip of his tongue to ask her. However, that was not why he was here.

"Hey, I take full responsibility for putting my foot in my mouth a few times since then, too," he said. "I've tried to make things right with you, but I don't know how. And at this point, it really doesn't matter if you resent me or think I'm a class-A jerk. I just need my girls to be in good hands. You're the only one I trust them with."

Her stony expression softened a fraction.

"I'd need you to watch them Monday through Friday. Obviously, I'd make it worth your while financially."

"I'm sorry, but no." She stood and crossed over to the window, rubbing her forearms as if chilled.

"What can I say that will convince you to agree?" He forced himself to stay seated.

"Nothing."

He'd hoped Eden would see this for what it was—a business arrangement—and agree. Maybe her dislike of him was stronger than he'd thought.

Had he been mistaken about her? Was she the best person to take care of his twins? When it came to women, he didn't always see clearly.

Still…his gut was telling him the girls needed Eden. And he'd do anything for his daughters.

She wanted to say yes.

Eden gripped her biceps as she stared unfocused out the window. Ryder's twins, Harper and Ivy, had wriggled into her heart the moment she'd met them over a year ago. But she had to decline. She was supposed to be working on her long-term plans, not drifting into another babysitting job.

"I don't have any other options." Ryder's caramel-brown eyes pierced hers. Why was he so handsome? She'd never been attracted to Mason in all the years she'd known him, but she found his identical twin, Ryder, to be positively gorgeous. It was strange.

"Have you even asked Martha if she'd babysit them full-time?"

"I don't want her to." Ryder sat with his knees spread, elbows on his thighs. His hands were clasped and dangling between his knees.

The man looked so muscular and lanky and miserable sitting on her couch it was all she could do not to go over there and pet his head like she had Mr. Jenkins's dogs.

"Martha has a lot of experience." Eden could not cave. She had her own life to live and would not get caught up in his problems. She'd gotten caught up in everyone else's problems for five years, and look where it had gotten her. "She used to take care of her grandkids."

"Martha doesn't have the energy or desire to watch lively preschoolers all day." He blew out a frustrated breath. "Is this about me? You wouldn't have to spend time with me or anything."

"This isn't about you." She didn't hate the guy. That being said, he was correct. He'd put his foot in his mouth on more than one occasion, but he probably didn't even know why she'd been offended. Eden would never forget the look on the twins' faces when he'd taken a phone call from his ex-wife at Christmas Fest and argued with her in front of them. They'd been devastated. When Eden pointedly told him she'd watch the girls if he got another call, he'd rudely told her to mind her own business. Then a few days later, he'd pulled her aside and told her she couldn't possibly understand since she'd never been married.

That one had hurt.

And over the past year, he'd made comment after comment about how she had the right idea by staying single.

As if it was by choice.

Ryder Fanning should come with a warning: *Hazard—Do Not Touch*. He was not the guy for her, and if she ever forgot it, even for a moment, all she had to do was picture his former wife, Lily Haviland, the glowing, talented, beautiful actress and winner of a Golden Globe.

Even if Ryder was the greatest guy on earth—which he wasn't—he would never be into ordinary Eden Page after being married to spectacular Lily Haviland. What man would?

"What is this about, then?" Ryder watched her with a thoughtful expression.

What was it about?

Getting her life together. For five years she'd been babysitting for her loved ones. She'd been happy to be there for them when they'd needed her the most. They were her friends, her support group.

But Ryder? He wasn't one of her friends. And she didn't want him to be.

Starting here, starting now, she was saying no.

"Taking care of the twins doesn't fit in with my plans."

He raked his fingers through short dark blond hair and met her eyes. "It would only be for the summer."

Harper and Ivy with their adorable dark wavy hair and gigantic blue eyes came to mind. They were darling girls. She could do the summer, couldn't she?

No. She wasn't getting sucked into his problems.

"Look, Lily's been out of the country shooting a movie," Ryder said. "The girls have been struggling since I told them we were moving. Ivy asks me roughly eighteen times a day how Mommy will find her when we move to Rendezvous. And Harper gets real quiet when

Lily is brought up. They need more care than the local day care center or Martha could give them."

Her heart ached for the poor girls. This wasn't just a move for them; it was a complete upheaval of their lives.

The day care would never do. And Martha was in her midsixties. It would be a lot for her to take care of the twins for hours every day. "My apartment isn't set up for multiple children."

"What are you talking about?" He stood and pointed to the dining area with all the toys. "You've got everything right there."

"But it would be cramped. I still babysit Phoebe a few times a week."

"They'll survive a few months of cramped. I'll pay you extra."

What else could she say? No argument came to mind.

"Well, I'd have to talk to Gabby," she said, caving. "She might not like the idea."

His face lit up. "Does this mean you'll do it?"

"I'll consider it. But if Gabby objects…"

"Thank you, Eden." He rose, crossed over and pulled her into a hug.

His arms were strong. In fact, the man was a wall of muscle. He smelled expensive, like department store cologne, and the overwhelming reality of him sent flutters to her stomach. She quickly stepped out of his embrace.

"Don't thank me yet. Gabby might say no." She doubted it, though. Gabby would probably rave about how Harper and Ivy would be like sisters to Phoebe.

"Why don't I get a pizza for us?" He grinned. "We can celebrate."

"Uh, no thanks. I have plans." The fib was necessary. Babysitting the girls was one thing. Pizza alone with him was another.

His grin faded away, but he cocked his chin to her. "Another time. Thanks, Eden. I'll see myself out."

After the door clicked shut behind him, she smashed a throw pillow into her chest. What was wrong with her? She'd done it again. Slid right into someone else's plans instead of concentrating on her own.

Was she being too hard on herself? She *did* want to babysit Harper and Ivy. They were going through a tough transition. It wasn't their fault she had issues with their father.

An uneasy feeling slithered down her spine. What if this wasn't about wanting to help the girls?

Ryder owned the ranch she grew up on.

He was single.

And alarmingly good-looking.

She'd have to be careful. Being around Ryder on a near-daily basis might revive her dream about getting married and raising a family on a ranch here in Rendezvous.

It had taken a long time to accept the dream wasn't going to happen.

The only one raising a family on the ranch would be Ryder, not her.

She'd try not to hold it against him.

Chapter Two

"I'm not going to regret this, am I?" The following Saturday, Ryder and the twins were official residents of Rendezvous. The moving company had unloaded the truck earlier, and a group of friends were helping him unpack. Ryder had been riding a wave of adrenaline all day, but now reality was setting in. It wasn't the first time he'd second-guessed his decision, but standing in the newly renovated living room of the farmhouse reminded him how permanent this move was.

"You did the right thing." Mason clapped him on the shoulder. "You said it yourself, you wanted a fresh start. A back-to-nature lifestyle to raise the girls."

"I do." He rubbed his chin. "I'm worried about them adapting."

"They sound happy to me." Mason arched his eyebrows, pointing to the ceiling where little footsteps pounded up and down the hallway accompanied by squeals and shouts. Noah and the girls were up there along with Mason's friends Gabby and Dylan Kingsley, who'd recently married and were supposed to be helping the twins unpack their toys. Not much unpacking could be happening with all that noise. If Ryder had to guess, he'd say they were playing tag. Or wrestling. Maybe both.

He dropped onto the couch and sighed.

"What's wrong?" Mason asked.

"I think it all kind of hit me. The weekends I've spent with you have helped me get a feel for cattle, but there's so much I don't know."

"Have you talked to Chris?" Mason asked. "He's been doing a good job managing this place since Bill and Joanna started traveling last year. He'll fill you in on everything you need to know. And I'm always here. Call anytime. That's what brothers are for."

Chris Ashbury had been doing a good job from what Ryder could tell, and he was thankful the man had agreed to stay on now that he owned the place.

"Thanks, Mason." Two years ago, he hadn't even known his identical twin existed. Now he relied on him for emotional support. "Chris does seem to know what he's doing."

"He does. He grew up around here working for local ranchers. Moved away a while back to get married. It's a shame he got divorced, but I'm glad he's back and ranching again."

Ryder had sunk a lot of money into buying this place, and he wanted everything right. He'd updated the farmhouse. Convinced Chris to work for him. And he'd landed the best babysitter possible for the girls. Eden had called earlier in the week and told him Gabby was okay with her babysitting all three children. So why was he having all these doubts?

"Has Eden been over yet?" Mason took in the room. "I can't get over the house. It's the same…but better."

"No, I invited her to come over tonight, but she's helping Nicole with the triplets." Ryder got up and opened a large box marked Living Room. Since he hadn't expected her to come over, it was stupid to be disappointed.

"Hey, Ryder," Brittany called from the kitchen. "Where do you want your pans?"

"Leave the man's pans alone," Mason yelled back. Brittany popped her head around the corner and stuck her tongue out at him, but the twinkle in her blue eyes teased.

"The cupboard next to the stove, please," Ryder said, then turned back to Mason "I appreciate you guys helping me out."

"We're glad to. Noah has been racing around like he scarfed down a bag full of candy he's been so excited to have Harper and Ivy living here." Mason dug through a box and held up two remote controls. "Media cabinet?"

Ryder nodded.

Gabby, looking flushed, came down the staircase with a big grin. "Eden is going to flip when she sees this place, Ryder."

"Why?" He hoped that was a good thing.

"The changes." The petite, curvy brunette waved her arm. "It's the same layout but so much brighter. And am I mistaken or did you find more room in the kitchen? It feels bigger, and it wasn't exactly small before."

"The kitchen was closed off, so I had the contractor bump out a wall and add an island. It's a better use of the space."

"Well, it's amazing." Gabby backed up several steps to peek through the sunroom. "Oh, good! You left the sunroom the same. I can't tell you how many times I've had tea and cookies in there with Eden and her mother. In fact, Phoebe learned to crawl in there. It's always been my favorite spot in the house."

An uncomfortable feeling prickled the back of Ryder's neck. Everyone kept mentioning Eden. He hadn't thought about her when he was renovating. She'd grown up here. Lived in this house until last year. She didn't like that he'd bought *her* ranch. How would she react when she saw the place? Would she resent the changes he'd made?

That was assuming she'd ever come over to see it. At this point, he doubted Eden would step foot in here.

Harper, Ivy and Noah raced down the stairs louder than wild beasts. Dylan slowly followed with an amused grin on his face. "I promised them sodas."

"There's caffeine-free soda in the cooler on the porch." Ryder hitched his thumb toward the front door, even though the last thing those three needed was more sugar.

"Daddy, guess what?" Ivy stopped in front of him, looking up through impossibly large dark blue eyes.

"What?" He crouched to her level.

She wrapped her arms around his neck. "I'm sleeping in Auntie Eden's room!"

The girls had often heard Noah refer to her as Auntie Eden, and they must have decided to call her that, too. He'd have to run it by her on Monday.

"It's not fair." Harper stormed up behind Ivy and crossed her arms over her chest in a major pout.

"What's not fair?" He turned his attention to her.

"I want to sleep in Auntie Eden's room! Why does Ivy get to and not me?"

Before Ryder could react, Mason picked up Harper, settling her on his hip. "Because you got Mia's room."

"Who's Mia?" She gave him her full attention.

"Noah's mother. She's Eden's sister. I was married to her, but she died when Noah was a baby."

"Miss Brittany's my mommy now, aren't you?" Noah puffed out his chest as Brittany joined them.

"I sure am." Brittany ruffled Noah's hair. "But your mother was a wonderful person from what I hear." Brittany directed her attention to Harper, still in Mason's arms. "You're the oldest, right?"

"Yes, I am." Harper threw a triumphant look Ivy's way. Ivy gave her the stink eye.

"Well, Mia was Eden's older sister. So it makes sense you would have her room."

"I'm younger, just like Auntie Eden." Ivy seemed pretty pleased with herself.

"Don't brag, Ivy." Harper turned back to Brittany. "Was Mia pretty?"

"She was real pretty." Noah stepped forward proudly. "You saw her. There's a picture on the wall in my house with Daddy and me when I was a baby."

"That's your mommy. I forgot." Harper hugged Mason's neck. "Uncle Mason, you look like Daddy, but you smell different."

Mason chuckled as he set her down. "Is that bad?"

"No, you smell good. Like clouds and air."

Mason met Ryder's gaze, and they both shrugged. Harper grabbed Noah's hand and they ran to the kitchen, announcing they were thirsty.

"Daddy?" Ivy had her worried face on again.

"What, pumpkin?"

"When is Mommy coming? Can she stay in my room?"

Ryder's heart sank. Ivy had been having a lot of separation anxiety in regard to Lily lately. *Lord, will You help me find the right words?* "She's shooting a movie in another country. Remember how I told you it's far away?"

"How come everyone else's mommies live with them and ours doesn't? It's not fair."

Ryder took Ivy by the hand and led her to the sunroom for privacy. He sat next to her on the small love seat.

"I know it's not fair, Ivy. But I can't do anything about

it. We aren't married anymore, and Mommy will visit when she can. Until then, we'll enjoy our new house and our new friends, okay?"

A tear dropped to her cheek and slid down her face. Then another.

"Aw, Ivy, don't cry. Your mommy loves you."

"Then why isn't she here?" She hiccupped.

Not having an answer for her, he pulled her into a tight hug. "You'll always have me. That's one thing I can promise."

"Ivy, I got you a orange pop!" Noah yelled.

She wiped her face and let out a pitiful sigh, then left the room to claim her soda.

He pinched the bridge of his nose. Maybe this move was going to be more difficult than he'd imagined. He'd asked Lily several times to visit the girls as soon as possible, and she'd said she would. But he knew her. If she planned a visit, something would come up—an amazing opportunity or a meeting she just had to take—and she'd either cancel the trip or cut it short.

In time the girls would come to terms with their mother's ways. But they were too young to understand at this point.

They wanted to be with her.

And she didn't want to be with them.

He would never put anything—or anyone—above his girls. Their needs came first. Everything else was a distant second. He wished Lily would put the girls first for once, too. But he doubted she ever would. And he'd be the one left to deal with the emotional fallout. As usual.

Her first day with the Fanning twins. Eden checked the side window again on Monday morning. Mrs. McNally was set to arrive any minute, and Eden didn't want her to have to navigate the stairs to the apartment. A silver minivan turned into the parking lot. Eden threw on her coat and headed down to get the girls.

Had she done the right thing by agreeing to babysit them?

It was too late to back out now, and frankly, she didn't want to. She'd make this transition as smooth as possible for them. Get to know them better. Then she'd be able to plan a schedule to keep them active, learning and engaged.

The sky was overcast, and the temperature had dropped overnight. She shivered as she approached the minivan idling in the spot next to the SUV her mom and dad gave her when they started traveling.

"Hi, girls!" Eden slid open the door and waved to them. They looked sleepy, but they both said hi. "Come on, let's get inside where it's warm."

After helping them out of the booster seats, she took their backpacks and thanked Martha. The girls waved as she drove away.

"This doesn't look like a house."

"It's not." Eden followed them up the stairs. "It's an apartment."

"Oh."

She opened the door and set their backpacks in the hall. "Go ahead and take off your shoes and coats. There are hooks in the closet for you."

The girls both had long brown hair with natural waves, big blue eyes and button noses. Eden sighed in relief when she saw that Ryder had pinned name tags on their sweaters. She thought she could tell them apart, but she wanted to be sure on the first day. Harper wore purple leggings with a green sweater featuring a purple puppy.

Ivy wore pink leggings with a baby-blue sweater featuring a pink kitten.

Eden gave them a quick tour of her place before leading them to the play area. They instantly gravitated to the play kitchen and doll furniture. Ivy selected a doll, and Harper began baking a pretend cake.

"Do you like your new house?" Eden sat cross-legged on the rug. As much as she didn't like the thought of anyone else living in her old home, she wanted them to be happy there.

"Yes, it's big. Auntie Eden, I sleep in your room!" With shining eyes, Ivy brought the doll over and set it in her lap. Cradling the baby, Eden melted at Ivy's sweetness.

"And I sleep in Mia's." Harper looked up from the pretend stove. "That's Noah's mommy."

"His *real* mommy," Ivy said.

Eden stifled a chuckle. "Yes, I know. Mia was my sister. And I'm glad you like your rooms."

"Mommy's going to come visit us soon." Ivy took the doll back and attempted to wrap it in a quilted blanket before placing it in the crib.

"How wonderful." It would be good for the girls to see their mother. Eden could picture Lily Haviland—not that she'd ever met the woman. She'd watched every episode of *Courtroom Crimes* Lily had starred in, and she'd seen most of her movies, too. The actress seemed so warm and kind and vivacious and beautiful. Eden couldn't imagine what it would be like to actually meet her. "We'll have to plan something nice for your mommy. We could do some projects. Then you'd have something to give her."

Rendezvous would likely be seeing a lot of Lily Haviland now that Ryder had arrived. She'd have to ask him when Lily planned on coming. It must be difficult for her to be away from the girls so much.

"Yay!" Ivy threw her hands in the air. "I want to give something special to Mommy."

"Of course." Eden ticked through her mental list of projects the girls could do. "What do you enjoy? Drawing? Painting?"

"Yes!" they shouted in unison.

Eden laughed. "Harper, why don't you make us a big chocolate cake while Ivy feeds the baby her bottle, and I'll get my binder of ideas out."

"I can only make pretend cake." Harper had a worried look in her eye.

"I don't have a bottle!" Ivy's tone held an edge of panic.

"Pretend cake is extra yummy, Harper." Eden pointed to the purple basket in the cubbies. "Bottles, bibs, diapers and everything the baby needs is in there, Ivy."

Harper took out a plastic mixing bowl and pretended to pour flour in it, while Ivy lined up the baby supplies. Eden took the opportunity to go to her bedroom closet where she kept binders of project ideas, worksheets and games for children. She brought two thick binders back to the play area.

"You better cover that baby, Ivy." Harper reached for the manual mixer. "When I beat this cake, stuff is going to go flying."

"Wait!" Ivy found a scarf to put over the crib. "Okay, she's safe."

Harper made buzzing noises as she cranked the pretend mixer, and Ivy clapped her hands. "You're doing it, Harper! I can't wait to have a big piece."

"Well, it has to go in the oven first or it'll be all soupy." She made a big production out of pouring the imaginary batter into a pan. Then she opened the plastic oven door, shoved the pan inside, kicked it shut and wiped her hands dramatically. "Ivy, that kid stinks. You better change its dipey."

The girl held the doll up, bottom first, and took a sniff. "Hooey." Ivy waved her hand in front of her nose and grabbed one of the Velcro diapers from the cubby.

Eden enjoyed their interaction. They played instinctively. Every now and then they'd argue over something, but they quickly resolved it and returned to their make-believe.

What a precious gift to watch these children play.

Poor Lily. She was missing it all.

Had she fought Ryder about bringing the girls here? She probably saw the twins often in LA. Why would Ryder move them so far away?

It was none of her business.

To be fair, he did have full custody of them. And he'd mentioned Lily was on location somewhere. Eden had no idea what their arrangement was. He didn't talk about his ex-wife. Ever.

"It's done!" Harper, with her arms covered to her elbows in oven mitts, flourished the pan.

"It so chocolatey." Ivy pretended to smell it.

"Harper, why don't you serve each of us a slice? And Ivy, the teapot is behind you. Let's have a tea party." Eden steepled her fingers below her chin. The girls' mouths formed Os as they hurried to the cubbies for the play dishes.

As they oohed and aahed over the imaginary cake, Ivy poured them pretend tea from the plastic teapot and Eden asked them about their favorite toys, activities and movies. Harper claimed she loved chasing butterflies, playing the running game—Eden wasn't sure she wanted to know what that entailed—and riding Daddy like a pony. Ivy, on the other hand, loved coloring, playing with her stuffed animals, and dressing Daddy up fancy with makeup and a feather scarf.

Eden hadn't pictured Ryder as the type to let the girls put makeup on him or ride him like a pony, but then, she didn't know him well. She really didn't know him at all.

"We should have a tea party with Daddy tonight," Ivy said to Harper.

"I'll bake another cake." Harper stretched her arm as high as it would go. "This big."

Eden wished she could freeze this moment in time. Five-year-old children were a lot of fun.

"Did you know I have a friend who's a real baker here in Rendezvous?" Eden said.

"Really?" Harper lifted shining eyes to her.

"Maybe we can talk her into letting us stop by one day so she can show you how she bakes."

"Oh, yes, I want to go!" Harper said.

"Do you know what else?" Eden asked.

"What?" They watched her with rapt attention.

"She has three babies. Triplets."

"Like us." Ivy pointed to Harper.

Harper nodded. "Except one more."

"And they're real babies?" Ivy asked, looking skeptical.

"Yes, they're real babies."

"Can we hold them?"

"I don't know," Eden said. "We'd have to ask permission."

"I'm not touching a real dipey." Harper furrowed her eyebrows and shook her head.

Eden laughed. "Don't worry. She'll handle the diapers. Now, I understand you girls have been going to preschool…"

For the next couple of hours, Eden had them do activities to determine their learning levels and interests. They were up to speed on their letters, colors, shapes and numbers.

After lunch, they began to argue more often. They were probably tired. The three of them snuggled on the couch and watched a Disney movie.

Her thoughts went to the upcoming week. Once again, she couldn't help thinking her apartment, while spacious enough for a single woman, was awfully small to babysit three children in. And she didn't want them to be cooped up all the time when the weather got nice, either.

Her own childhood on the ranch had been wonderful. She and Mia would run around their big backyard, ride horses with their dad and help their mom bake and cook in the kitchen. The ranch had given her freedom, space, family and more.

She stole a peek at the girls on either side of her.

She wanted them to have a childhood like hers. Not stuck in an apartment while their mother was far away and their dad was working cattle.

It wasn't up to her, though.

There was nothing she could do about it, but it bothered her just the same.

"Daddy! Daddy!" The twins raced to Ryder after Eden let him into her apartment later that afternoon. They hung on his legs, both talking at once. Their happy faces pushed away the troubles of the day and took the edge off his doubts about making such a drastic life change.

"Easy does it. One at a time." He put his hands up in surrender, and they let go of his legs to hop up and down.

"We had a tea party, and I'm going to make you the biggest cake ever." Harper propped her little fists under her chin in excitement.

"I like cake." He was used to Harper being the first to jump in with whatever was on her mind. The kid tended to do everything heart first, head later. Her enthusiasm made life sweet, even if it did give him heart palpitations at times.

"I poured the tea." Ivy spun in a little circle. "And we watched a movie with kitties, and I want a fluffy white kitten so I can put a pink bow around her neck and she can sleep with me every night."

That was his Ivy. Always wanting a kitten. Now that they were living in the country, he could probably make it happen. The barn cats weren't tamed or he'd bring one of them inside for her.

"Sounds like you had a good day." He met Eden's eyes then, and his pulse roared to life. She was actually smiling. Man, she was pretty when she smiled.

"We made lots of pictures, Daddy." Harper took his hand and dragged him to the dining area. "See?"

He took in the table full of drawings and craft projects.

"We did our small letters, too." Ivy took his other hand and pointed to the stack of paper lined for handwriting.

"You were busy." Real busy. He couldn't believe they'd done so much in one day. They typically colored a picture or two with the nanny back in LA. That was it.

"You can take these with you, girls." Eden had paper clipped two piles, one for Ivy and one for Harper. "The other ones we'll bind into books for you to give to your mother when she comes to visit."

"Yay!" Ivy cheered. "I can't wait to show it to Mommy."

"Me, too!" Harper said.

Their mother? He wasn't sure why Eden was having them make books for her, but if it made the twins happy… "Well, girls, get your coats on while I talk to Eden a minute."

They raced to the closet at the end of the hall.

"I can't believe you did all this." Ryder looked at the table again. "You're really organized. I'm impressed."

"It's nothing." Her lips were still curved, making her look young, happy, serene. "I enjoyed it. Harper and Ivy are delightful. But I'd better warn you I don't know how much we'll be able to get done on their special books before Lily arrives. I'll do my best."

"What do you mean?" Was he missing something? She acted like Lily was coming in two days.

"I'll have the girls do some finger painting, collages, drawings, that sort of thing. We can include some of their letters and numbers, too, if you'd like."

"Lily isn't—" He realized the girls were standing behind him. He straightened his spine. "She'll love them."

"Great." Eden handed each girl her backpack. "Maybe we can talk later. I have a few questions, and I want you to have time to consider them before giving me your answers."

"Should I be concerned?" He guided the girls down the hallway.

"No, it's about field trips."

"Field trips? Oh. Okay." He opened the door. "Tell Miss Eden thank you."

"Thank you, Auntie Eden," they chimed, giving her a big hug. Then they held hands, went outside and made their way down the staircase, holding on to the rail and laughing all the way.

"Do you mind if they call you Auntie Eden?" He paused on the landing. "They picked it up from Noah."

"Not at all."

"I'll call you after supper. We can discuss the field trips and…whatever."

"Sounds good." She began to shut the door, and he had to force himself to move forward. It had been a long, hard day, and he wanted nothing more than to tell her about it. But they weren't friends, not really. And she was already doing him a big favor.

"Hey, Ryder," she said.

"Yeah?" He turned back, hope rumbling through his chest.

"Get some rest. Ranching this time of year, well, it's not easy with all the new calves."

"Thanks, Eden. I will." His spirits bounced back as he descended the steps. Maybe she didn't hate him. It was a start in the right direction at least. And working with those calves had been exhausting.

The girls stood next to his truck, and he opened the door and lifted each of them into it. Once they got settled in their booster seats, he checked to make sure they were buckled properly. Then he climbed into the driver's seat and fired the engine.

"Who wants burgers?" he asked.

"Me! Me!" they shouted.

Good, because he didn't have an ounce of energy left to cook.

Later that evening after the twins had conked out in their beds, Ryder sat on the couch in sweatpants and a long-sleeved T-shirt. It was the first moment he'd had to digest his day, and he'd rather forget it ever happened.

Right away he and Chris had fed and checked the cattle, then moved on to other chores. It seemed as if every five minutes ten new questions came to mind. They'd gone over the calendar so he'd know what to expect, and then Chris had excused himself to work on a busted piece of machinery. Ryder had left himself voice memo after voice memo of things to check into, and he still felt clueless even after studying the previous six months of books that Bill Page, Eden's father, had graciously left for him.

To say he was overwhelmed would be the understatement of the century.

He scrolled through his phone, noting the seventeen voice memos he'd left for himself, and decided they could wait. It was high time he called Eden. She answered on the third ring.

"I hope I'm not interrupting anything." He held his breath, anticipating a snippy reply.

"Nope." She sounded friendly. Huh. There was a first time for everything. "I'm so bored I'm watching a television special on what causes crop circles."

He chuckled. "Crop circles, huh? Any answers?"

"Besides teenage pranksters? No."

"Want me to let you go? I'd hate for you to miss anything."

Her laugh was a melody to his ears. "Watching this program is a new low for me. How are the girls? Did they seem okay tonight?"

Wait. Was he having an actual conversation with Eden? The woman who'd refused to give him the time of day since they'd met?

"They're great. They wouldn't stop talking all through supper. You must have tired them out, though, because neither one gave me any grief about bath time or going to bed."

"I'm glad. They're amazing little girls."

Hearing her praise his babies filled his chest with pride. He loved those kids, but he worried he was failing them. The women in their lives hadn't been very reliable.

Lily refused to share custody. She visited them when it suited her, which wasn't often. And every nanny Ryder hired had left for greener pastures within six months.

Eden continued. "I wondered if you'd be okay with me taking the girls to the library once or twice a week. I also thought they'd like to have a baking session with Nicole. It would give them a chance to see the triplets. This morning, Harper zoomed over to the play kitchen, and Ivy clearly loves babies. I think it would be fun for them both."

Gratitude flooded him. In one day, Eden had recognized Harper's and Ivy's different interests and wanted to make a special outing for them.

The woman was something.

All the ways Lily had misled him rushed back. She'd wanted kids right away, wanted to stay home with them, wanted to take a break from acting.

He'd thought Lily was something, too.

Until she'd proven him so spectacularly wrong.

"That would be great." He wasn't going to judge Eden based on Lily's behavior. "You have my permission to take them wherever you'd like. As long as it's local, I'm fine with it."

"Don't worry. I don't have any overnight stays planned at this point." There it was again—Eden teasing. He wouldn't have thought it possible a week ago. "On a serious note, though, I'll let you know ahead of time if we're planning something out of the ordinary."

"I appreciate it. But if it's a matter of going to the park or library or whatever, don't feel like you need my permission." He realized he hadn't discussed her expense account. He always gave the nanny a credit card to buy the girls' lunches or to go out and have some fun. "By the way, I have a credit card for you to use. For, you know, if you want to go out to lunch or grab some Dipping Dream ice cream."

"That isn't necessary, Ryder."

"It is." He wasn't going to have her pay for his children's fun. And he also needed to clear the air about Lily visiting. He wasn't sure why Eden assumed she was coming soon, but he figured the girls had said something. "Earlier you mentioned making books for Lily."

"Is that a problem?" Her tone shifted from friendly to ice-cold in an instant. He already missed the banter they'd been enjoying.

"No, not at all. It's thoughtful of you. But Lily isn't coming right away."

"When is she coming?"

He raked his hand through his hair. Lily was a touchy subject between him and Eden. He didn't want to make things awkward. He'd have to choose his words carefully.

"She's been on location in New Zealand. I'm not sure when shooting wraps up or when she'll be able to get away."

"Oh, I see."

From her quiet answer, he doubted she saw at all. But what was the point in setting her straight? He'd accepted that Lily Haviland's number-one priority in life was herself. She wasn't a bad person. She said the right things when she came around, but she'd let him and the girls down too many times to count.

He had no faith in his ex-wife at all. But it would do the girls no good for him to bad-mouth their mother to Eden or anyone. It wouldn't do him any good, either. A lot of prayer had helped him get to this point, and he wasn't about to backslide now.

"When I have a firm date, I'll let you know," he said.

"Okay."

What could he say to get them back to a good place? "I guess this means it will give the girls more time to make the books."

"Yes." Her voice brightened. "I'll come up with some fun projects for them. Don't you worry."

Like he'd ever worry with her in charge of the girls. He'd seen her close relationship with Noah. And she always seemed to be babysitting for her friends whenever he came to town. She had a special touch when it came to children.

He'd been right to hire Eden. She was the dream babysitter every parent longed for. In her capable hands, his girls would be all right. He just had to be careful on a personal level. Eden didn't seem to like him much, anyhow. But if she changed her mind about him…he'd be tempted to explore the possibilities with her.

The truth was he didn't know Eden all that well.

And it was best if he kept it that way.

Chapter Three

This arrangement wasn't working.

The following Saturday morning, Eden bit into a cinnamon roll as she strolled to the park. She'd stopped for coffee and picked up the pastry on her way to meet Ryder. The first day of May held the scent of possibility, or maybe it was the smell of the grass coming back to life after a snowy winter. Either way, the sun was shining.

The blue skies would help her deliver bad news. It would be cruel to hurt someone, even Ryder, on a gray day.

A white gazebo ahead encouraged her to *come on in*, but she decided to sit at a picnic table on the lawn to let the sun warm her face. The temperature was still cool enough to need her winter coat. At least she'd been able to leave her hat and gloves behind.

For the past three days she'd been trying to come up with a solution to her babysitting problem. Her apartment was too small for the children. And late in the afternoon, music from the dance studio below distracted the girls. Eden had learned to tune it out ages ago, but on the days Brittany held classes, the twins, already tired, struggled to pay attention and grew ornery.

If only Eden still lived on the ranch. It had been perfect for babysitting. The rambling farmhouse had a large family room in addition to the other common areas. Eden and Mia had played a million games in there, and more recently, Eden had spent many special days with Mia's son in there. She and Noah had read stories, played games and made too many crafts to count. When the weather was nice, they'd always go outside.

She couldn't imagine what the farmhouse looked like now. Her chest crumbled like an old sponge. She missed it. The day she'd said goodbye to it had been a low point for her. All the memories of Mia and her childhood were wrapped up in those walls. Were the pencil lines in the closet where Dad had measured them each year still there?

"Nice day, isn't it?"

She hadn't noticed Ryder striding up. His broad grin made her stomach drop like the first hill of a roller coaster. He wore loose-fitting jeans and a Henley under an unzipped jacket. A cowboy hat covered his hair.

"It is." Now that he was here, she had no idea what to say. She wanted to babysit the girls, but she didn't see how she could continue. Three small children bouncing off one another was stressful, and she couldn't continue to put them through an hour of music blaring at the precise time they were most tired.

"I take it you have something on your mind." He weaved his legs into the picnic table to sit opposite her.

Usually looking at his face turned her insides mushy, but the bags under his eyes and his drawn cheeks concerned her. He looked exhausted. And dejected. He was clearly making an effort to hide his mood behind a smile.

"Rough first week on the ranch?" she asked gently.

"Why?" His eyebrows drew together. "Did someone say something?"

"No, you look tired, that's all."

"Oh." He ran his hand down his cheek. "I guess I am."

"Not used to getting up at the crack of dawn to check cattle, are you?"

"It's getting easier." With that he yawned. "It is, really. Ignore that."

"What are you doing about night checks?" Funny, she hadn't considered how being a single dad on the ranch would affect calving. Her father had gone out at all hours of the night to check pregnant cows. His calving season began in March, was heaviest in April and finished in May. Cold weather and late storms always affected the herd. She hoped they wouldn't get more snow.

"I hired two people to take shifts in the night. Charlie agreed to stay on through June. Naomi might, too."

"Smart. That way you won't have to leave Harper and Ivy alone." She wondered if it bothered him to not be out there checking the cattle himself, though.

"Exactly. I'm thankful for the extra help. The cows…" His lips drew together in a tight line.

"What's wrong with them?" She ticked through the various cattle issues her father had dealt with over the years. Malnutrition, freezing to death, losing newborn calves, predators…

"Everyone can see I'm new at this, including the cows." His jaw shifted, then he met her eyes and his expression softened. "Some of those new moms are ornery."

"Don't I know it." She stared off into the distance as the memories came back. "Dad used to come in cussin' up a storm when he had to deal with a protective mama cow."

His mouth curved upward but fell just as quickly.

She'd helped Dad with the cattle until she graduated high school. It wasn't her favorite thing in the world, but spending time with him and the ranch hands had taught her many tricks about raising cattle in the harsh Wyoming climate. She'd helped out in almost any situation whenever the need arose.

"I know raising cattle is new for you," she said, "but the rest of it isn't. You grew up in Montana, right? So you're used to the weather. And raising sheep means you had to deal with a lot of the same things we do. Keeping them safe, fed and alive are the top priorities. Don't worry. You'll get it."

He met her eyes then, and she took a sharp intake of breath at the gratitude radiating from them. He must have had a rough week if a few sentences of encouragement from her were helping him.

"You sure about that?" he asked. "I feel about as green as a new blade of grass, and everyone who works for me can see it, too."

"Oh, don't worry. They'll think you're an amateur for a while." She'd seen the way they teased each other. Cowboys had to earn respect in these parts, even when they owned the ranch. "They'll respect you eventually. How bad is it?"

"I'll survive."

"By this time next year, you'll not only be the boss, but they'll look at you like one, too."

"Yeah, well, I hope by this time next year, I'll be worthy of their respect. I almost lost a calf yesterday, and I haven't stopped thinking about it. How can anyone look up to their boss if he can barely keep a fresh-born calf alive?"

"What happened?" Her forgotten coffee stood to the side, and she sipped it, still warm, as he shook his head.

"I drove the UTV to a group of cows with a bunch of calves born during the past two weeks. There in the middle of them was a mother and a fresh calf next to her. The baby was kneeling on his front legs and not getting up."

"She had the baby right in the middle of them?" Eden frowned. "Something must have been off."

"You think so?" He shrugged one shoulder. "Anyhow, I went up to it, and the mama took a step back—"

"Wait, she let you draw near without a fuss?"

"Yeah, she stayed close to the calf, but she let me check him out."

"Something really must have been off," she muttered. Pregnant cows usually separated from the other cattle to have their babies, and they typically pawed at the ground to protect the calf when someone came near.

"Well, I tagged him and tried to get him to stand, but he couldn't support himself. I didn't know what to do. I was going to leave him, figuring the mother would take charge, but I kept thinking something wasn't right. Last week I witnessed a dozen births, and none of them were like this. I hemmed and hawed for a good ten minutes and finally called Chris. He told me to take him to the calf warmer in the shop. After a couple of hours, Chris weighed him, got him on his feet, and I took him back to his mom. He was still pretty wobbly."

"Did he nurse?"

"Yeah. He's okay now. But I didn't even think of getting him to the warmer." He shook his head in disgust. "Chris told me he was quite a bit larger than most of our calves, and the mother probably struggled to give birth to him. The little guy might not have had the energy to stand."

For the past year, she'd believed Ryder thought only about himself, but this version of him wasn't lining up with the one in her head. This Ryder wasn't egotistical. He cared about the cattle, and he was humble enough to admit he needed help. "Well, now you know."

"True. But what else don't I know that could affect the herd? I'd hate to lose a calf due to my lack of knowledge."

"You have plenty of ranch hands and a brother a few miles down the road. You don't have to be an expert right now." She almost reached over to cover his hand but stopped herself. What would possess her to consider such a thing? She wasn't going to voluntarily touch him.

"Thanks, Eden. I needed the pep talk." His face had more color, and he didn't look as tired. "Now, what did you want to discuss?"

She mentally cringed. How could she kick a guy when he was down?

What was the alternative, though? For years she'd accommodated her friends when they needed her even when it wasn't ideal for her, and the accommodation needed to stop.

I can't keep going along with other people's plans because it's good for them. It needs to be good for me, too.

"My apartment is too small to watch the girls," she said. "This isn't working out."

As if he didn't have enough problems… Ryder slumped. Between the ranch hands exchanging raised eyebrows at his inexperience, his own high expectations of sliding into the role of cattle rancher, and the girls waffling between highs and lows, the one highlight of the move had been not worrying about the twins while Eden watched them. And now she wasn't going to?

She had to.

He couldn't let her quit.

"Okay, we'll come up with a solution." His mind raced in circles like a dog chasing its tail. "Space is the issue?"

She looked down at her coffee cup. "It's not the only one."

"Is it the girls? Are they acting up?" A fire roared in his core. They'd always been affectionate, happy children. Sure, Harper could be high energy, and Ivy sulked for reasons he'd never understand, but all in all, they were good kids. Weren't they?

"No, of course not, they're wonderful." She sounded so offended; the fire inside him immediately doused. "No, it truly is my space or lack of it. Kids their age need room to run and move. They're bouncing off the walls and off each other. My table is too small for their art projects, and the days Brittany has classes, the music comes straight up to my apartment. It bothers the twins, and I hate seeing them ornery because of it."

"So, watch them at my place." Problem solved. The tension gripping his neck relaxed.

Her face went completely blank. Grew a tad green. "I couldn't."

"Why not?"

"It's…" She appeared to be struggling for words. "I have Phoebe, too."

"So?" He didn't mind her babysitting Gabby's little girl at his house. "My ranch is closer to Dylan and Gabby's new home than your place anyhow. What's the problem?"

"It's not happening." The words came out rapid-fire.

"Why not?"

"It would be too weird."

Was she worried about being alone on the ranch with him? She had nothing to fear. He was so busy checking cattle, feeding them, coming up with spreadsheets to track their nutrition and trying to keep up with repairs that he could barely breathe.

"We wouldn't be alone." He held his palms out. "And even if we were, you wouldn't have to worry about me. I've got two priorities—the girls and my ranch. I'm never getting married again, either, so rest easy."

"That's not what I was talking about." Her expression had a horrified tinge to it. "I'm not interested in you like that. I mean, you're the identical twin of my brother in law. Do you really think I'd ever be attracted to someone who looks exactly like my dead sister's husband? Ew."

Put in those terms…

He stretched his neck from side to side. Eden had never found him attractive? He could see her point—she'd been related to Mason before her sister died. And their friendship had continued for years. But he wasn't Mason, even if he was his double.

And Ryder was definitely attracted to Eden. Had been from the minute he'd met her.

It was just as well. Attraction could lead to more dangerous emotions—like love. And he wasn't doing *that* again.

She shivered, burrowing deeper into her jacket.

"Are you cold?" he asked. "We can take this to Riverview Lounge where it's warmer."

"I'm fine."

A long silence stretched. He kept turning over the fact she wasn't interested in him and didn't find him attractive because of Mason. The idea wouldn't have occurred to him in a million years. Strangely enough, it was like dangling forbidden fruit in front of him.

"What are you doing today?" He'd dropped Harper and Ivy off at Mason's to play with Noah this morning so he could meet Eden here. He figured once he was done, he'd take the girls on a ride around the ranch. Show them all the calves and cows. They'd love it. But with Eden giving him a hard time about babysitting…maybe it was time he brought her to the ranch. Let her see for herself it was the perfect solution to her space problem.

"I have plans." She sat primly with her hands in her lap.

"What kind of plans?"

"Plans that are none of your business."

Her closed-off tone matched her closed-off expression. He missed the ray of friendship she'd shown him mere moments ago.

"Why don't you like me, Eden?"

"I like you." It sounded weak.

"Never mind. You don't have to like me. I just—the girls need you. Come to the house. Look it over and tell me if it will work for babysitting."

"I can't."

"Can't or won't?"

"Both."

She was honest. He'd give her that.

"Why?"

"Because it's too hard." Only then did he notice how much emotion she seemed to be bottling in. "It was… home."

The word was infused with reverence, longing and loss. He knew she'd been living with her parents until last year. He'd assumed she'd moved into the apartment above Brittany's studio to get some independence. Now he wasn't so sure.

"I don't know what to say. Your parents were selling it. I feel like I should apologize, but I'm not sure what I'd be apologizing for."

She ducked her chin, avoiding his eyes.

"If you come over, you'll see it's got plenty of room for all three of the kids." Ryder couldn't afford to lose her—neither could the twins. "The big room in the back is practically empty. You can order any furniture and supplies you need. I'll pay for them."

"Noah and I spent a lot of time in the family room when I babysat him." Her thoughtful expression was like when the sun peeked through the clouds. Full of light.

"See? You already know what to do with it." He uncurled his legs from the bench, rounded the table and held out his hand. "The girls are at Mason's. Come on. I'll take you to the ranch. At least look it over before you say no to babysitting there."

Ignoring his hand, she stood. "I don't want to babysit at your house."

"It was your home. I get it. I can't change that."

"I'm not asking you to." Gone was her feisty tone, replaced by resignation.

"Then what's the problem?"

"It's complicated."

"I need you, Eden. Harper and Ivy need you. This move has been hard, and you're making it easy on them. And on me."

Eden rubbed her temples, then exhaled loudly. "Fine. You win. I'll babysit at your place. Starting Monday morning."

"This isn't about winning or losing. It's about solving a problem."

"Well, it feels like losing to me."

"I don't want you to feel that way. I mean, if there's any other thing you can think of—I want to work this out…" He didn't know what would make her happy.

"There isn't. You're right. It will be easier on everyone."

He could practically hear the words *except me* at the end.

"It might feel less win or lose if I give you the tour."

"No thanks." She stood.

"At least let me drop you off at your place." He hitched his chin toward his truck parked behind them.

"I'll walk."

As she turned to leave, he didn't feel like a winner, either. Maybe this was a lose-lose for both of them. The fact was he liked confiding in Eden. Had needed her encouragement about the ranch. And now a wall was up—a wall because of him.

He should be happy about it.

Eden was uncomplicated with everyone but him. He should let her build as many walls as she needed to keep an emotional distance between them.

Yeah, right.

The more walls she built, the more he'd want to tear them down. In fact, if he knew himself at all, he'd make sure every one of her walls were rubble before summer was over. And then where would he be?

He couldn't go through another heartbreak. Instead of worrying about her walls, he'd be smart to erect a few of his own.

Chapter Four

The moment she'd been dreading had finally arrived. Eden trudged up the walkway to the front porch of her childhood home Monday morning and stopped before the porch steps. The weather had grown nasty overnight with freezing temperatures and gusty winds. The cold struck her cheeks, but she barely noticed. What if she went inside and the changes to her home were too much? What if she had an emotional meltdown in front of the twins?

The porch was full of shadows from the past. She could practically see her and Mia sitting side by side on the top step, each holding a doll and debating whether to take their babies on a picnic by the creek or leave them here and go pick wildflowers for their mother.

Why did you have to die, Mia? Her big sister had been her hero, her second mom, her best friend. And this house—like everything else around here—had moved on as if Mia never existed.

Eden forced her feet up the steps and, shivering, rang the doorbell. It would be just her and the twins today, since Gabby didn't need her to babysit Phoebe on Mondays. Martha was still driving here early to get the girls up and fed while Ryder tackled ranch chores. The front door opened, and instead of Martha, Ryder appeared. His hair was rumpled, and he wore a sweatshirt, jeans and bare feet. Seeing his toes felt oddly intimate.

"Hey," he said. His eyes brightened as his mouth curved into a self-deprecating smile.

"Hey."

He opened the door wide, and she went inside, trying to avoid brushing against him. In the foyer, she stooped to take off her boots, then slid off her coat. Ryder took it from her and hung it up in the hall closet.

"I thought you'd be out feeding cows or something." She clutched a tote full of supplies for the day.

"I wanted to be here to thank you and to give you the tour."

"You don't need to…"

"Yes, I do."

"I don't want—"

"You told me you didn't want your parents to sell this place." He made no effort to move from the foyer. "I know it's important to you, and I want you to feel comfortable here."

Everything he said was true, but he didn't get it. This was more than her childhood home. It held her memories of her sister, and she would never have the opportunity to make new ones.

"Auntie Eden!" Harper raced down the hall and wrapped her arms around Eden's legs. Then she stared up at her through those big blue eyes. "You're here! I'm gonna show you my room!"

Mia's room. Eden's heart lurched, but she attempted to smile as she smoothed Harper's hair. "I would love that."

Ryder's cell phone rang. "Mind giving me a sec? It's Chris."

"Go ahead." Eden let Harper take her hand and was soon dragged to the staircase.

"I'm coming, too!" Ivy bounced down the hall to them as they reached the first step.

Eden glanced back at Ryder, who frowned as he talked to Chris. "No…yeah. Okay, I see your point. We'll keep an eye on her throughout the day…thanks for the heads-up."

"Everything okay?" she asked. The girls yanked on her arms to keep going upstairs.

"I think so. We still have some pregnant cows to check after last night's storm."

"Go ahead. We'll be fine." Eden held her breath, hoping he'd take the hint and leave them alone. She didn't want him around to witness her reaction. *Dear Lord, please help me hold it together in front of the girls.*

"If you're sure…" He hesitated, then nodded. "Text or call if you need anything."

"Come on, Auntie Eden!" The girls pulled her forward.

"Okay, okay, don't rip my arms off." She laughed, but dread bubbled in her gut.

At the top of the stairs, she paused. Everything had been freshly painted in pale gray with white trim. It seemed bigger than before. The girls began arguing over which room to show Eden first.

"Which room is closest?" It wasn't difficult to neutralize their tempers. Harper grudgingly admitted Ivy's was, so they went in there first.

As soon as Eden walked in, the dread vanished. The room was painted pale pink, and it had new carpet. Ivy's bed took up a big portion of the room, and a white desk and white dresser rounded out the furniture. Bookcases were lined with toys and books, and stuffed animals sat on the top. The room was precious.

"I love it, Ivy." And she did. Eden's memories of flopping onto her stomach on the floor, paging through a picture book and petting her beloved orange cat, Muffin, were still here despite the fresh paint and new furniture. "Do you?"

"Yes," Ivy said. "Daddy tucks me in every night and hugs Fluffybear extra tight."

"Who is Fluffybear?"

Harper raced to the bed and lugged a big floppy stuffed bear over. "He's right here. Ivy's not 'llowed to take him out."

"Harper! I wanted to show her."

"Sorry." Harper didn't sound sorry.

"Can I give him a hug?" Eden held her arms out, and Ivy took Fluffybear from Harper and pressed him into her arms. She could smell the faint scent of fabric softener and a whiff of Ryder's cologne as she lingered over it a second more than she should have. "Why don't you show me everything else?"

Ivy conducted the tour of the room, pointing out the special toys her mother had bought her and a framed picture of Lily crouching with her arms around the twins' shoulders. Her beauty stopped Eden cold. Ryder's ex-wife's skin was flawless, her eyes big and blue, her hair long and brown, the same as the twins'. Her groomed eyebrows, straight nose and full lips were perfection. She appeared kind, happy, outgoing.

"I want Mommy to stay in my room when she comes," Ivy said.

"That's not fair." Harper frowned.

Ivy got close to her sister and looked her in the eyes. "She can sleep with me one night and you the next."

Harper's face cleared. "Okay."

"Are you ready to show me your room?" Eden asked Harper.

They made their way down the hall to Harper's room. Mia's old room. Eden's heart pinched as strains of Mia's laughter echoed in her mind.

"C'mon." The girls ran ahead of her, and she took a moment to prepare herself. How many times had Mia slammed the door shut in her face when they were young and mad at each other? How many times had they played with their Barbies in there? Listened to music? Giggled about boys and friends? When Mia was a senior, she'd pulled Eden inside and shut the door. Her face had positively dazzled as she told her Ben Jones had asked her to prom. The high school quarterback! And so cute. They'd jumped up and down and discussed it all night.

That was what hurt the most about Mia being gone. She missed their bond. Missed the one person who knew all her secrets. She'd shared everything with Mia.

"Aren't you comin' in?" Harper's forehead wrinkled in concern.

"Of course I am." Eden forced a happy expression on her face. It wasn't Harper's fault she was struggling today, and even if she had to fake it, she'd ooh and aah over her room.

Eden entered the butter-yellow room with the same furniture as Ivy's. Harper's was messier. Plastic horse figurines lay on their sides in front of the bookshelf, and three rumpled shirts had been tossed near the closet. A pile of books had toppled over by the bed.

"Why'd you look so sad?" Harper asked.

"Did I?" The girls were more perceptive than she realized. "You know this was my sister's room, right?"

"Uh-huh."

"I miss her. I have a lot of good memories with her in here."

Harper took Eden's hand and pressed it to her own cheek. "I'm sorry you miss her."

Ivy snuggled up against Eden's side. "I'm sorry, too, Auntie Eden."

Such sweet girls.

"I guess it would be strange if we didn't miss the people we love, wouldn't it?" She put her arms around them and hugged them both.

"I miss Mommy." Ivy sighed.

"Me, too." Harper's face couldn't droop any farther.

"Of course, you do. Just because she isn't here doesn't mean she doesn't love you." Eden had an idea. "Why don't I take pictures of you in your new rooms? We can add them to your special books for when she visits. Then when she misses you, all she has to do is open the books."

Both girls turned to each other and grinned. "Yes!"

For the next twenty minutes, Eden took pictures of the girls in every room of the house, except Ryder's bedroom. Finally, they ended up in the kitchen. As they wrapped up the tour, Eden marveled at the changes. The house was the same—but different. Brighter. More open. Still full of love.

"When it gets nice out, we can go on adventures around the ranch." Eden poured each girl a glass of milk. "I know all kinds of hidden places."

"You do?"

"I do. And pretty soon there will be wildflowers along the creek. You can pick them and make bouquets."

"I love flowers," Ivy said with a dreamy expression.

"I want to ride horseys." Harper had a milk mustache.

"What about you, Ivy?" Eden asked. "Do you want to ride a horse?"

"I don't know. They're big."

"I learned to ride when I was around your age." Eden had practically grown up riding. "I think you'll like it."

As the afternoon wore on, Eden felt more and more at home in her old house. And as she helped the girls glue cotton balls to construction-paper sheep, Eden couldn't help thinking she owed Ryder an apology. He'd bought the ranch and made the old farmhouse even better than it was before. Plus, because of him, the property was still being used to raise cattle. Her dad had worried that without the right buyer the ranch might cease to exist.

By coming here and seeing the house through Harper's and Ivy's eyes, Eden had finally gotten a sense of peace about letting go of the ranch. Her sister's memory wasn't being erased. Mia would always be with Eden. And the house would now hold Harper's and Ivy's memories in addition to hers and Mia's.

A tiny voice in her head whispered *Ryder is single. You could have it all—the house, the ranch, the family.*

No. She wasn't going down that road. She'd be nicer to Ryder and leave it at that. The stirrings and whispers inside her would disappear when summer ended. At least she hoped they would.

"Next week?" Ryder leaned back in the rickety office chair and glanced at the desk in the pole barn office while he talked to Lily on the phone. Since she rarely returned his calls and almost never picked up, he'd forced himself to take her call.

He still had to check a pregnant cow one more time before relieving Eden of her babysitting duties. The clock showed he was already late. All he wanted to do was find out how her first day of babysitting here had gone and make sure she was still willing to watch the girls here on the ranch. But no, he was going to be even later because he had to deal with Lily.

"I'm back in LA to promote my new movie, so I figured next week would be ideal to come see my sweethearts."

He clenched his jaw. *Don't be a jerk to her. You're better than that.* "They'll love seeing you. They've both been talking about you nonstop and can't wait to show you their new rooms."

There. He'd managed to keep his tone civil. Pleasant, even.

The long pause made him wonder if she'd heard him. Then her silky voice came through. "Perfect."

"When do you think you'll arrive? We have a guest room. You can stay here if you'd like."

"I'll have Mandy make the arrangements. Something in town will be fine." Her voice grew muffled as she called to her personal assistant, Mandy Drake, to check flights. Ryder had spent more time talking to Mandy over the past two years than to Lily herself.

"You know there aren't any direct flights here, right?" he asked. "You'll have to drive in from the nearest airport, and it's not close."

"I've been to remote places on location, Ryder. I can handle it." Her laugh was rich, and he tried to remember a time when he'd loved hearing it. He supposed it was before he realized it wasn't genuine. She used it as a prop.

"When you nail down the details, let me know." He tapped a pen against the desk and checked the clock again. "I'm not telling the girls unless you're one hundred percent sure you're coming."

"Why wouldn't I come?"

"I don't know. You tell me."

"I don't appreciate your tone. You act like I don't want

to visit them. I'm the one making these plans, so I don't know why you're being like this."

He took a deep breath before answering. "I appreciate you making the effort. Like I said, call or text me the details after Mandy gets everything booked."

"Will do. Oh, my publicist did mention the possibility of a guest appearance while I'm in town, though. I'm sure nothing will come of it."

Ryder's blood pressure climbed. He wasn't going to say a thing. Not one thing. As soon as she'd uttered that nonchalant *oh*, he'd known the visit wasn't going to happen. If the sun stood still, maybe he'd get confirmation that Mandy had booked a flight and reserved a room here in Rendezvous. But until then, he wasn't mentioning it to the girls. Their hopes had been shattered too many times by Lily already.

"Gotta go," Lily said. "Give the girls hugs and kisses from me."

He didn't respond, and the line went dead.

Leaning way back in the chair with his hands behind his head, he tried to erase the conversation. But he couldn't, and the longer he sat there, the more his anger rose. What was the point in her calling him if she was only going to make empty promises?

Lurching to his feet, he grabbed his hat and shoved the cell phone into his pocket. Then he locked up and marched down the gravel lane to the house. In the mudroom, he pulled off his boots, hung up his coat and washed his hands. By the time he finished, his mood had improved enough to find Eden and the girls.

He made his way through the hallway leading to the kitchen.

And he stopped short. Behind the island, Eden was laughing. Both girls sat on stools, giggling as they had a sword fight with breadsticks. The aroma of garlic and spaghetti sauce filled the air. His stomach immediately began to growl.

"Well, this is more than I ever imagined coming home to." He kissed Ivy's cheek, then Harper's. Then he met Eden's eyes. "I'm real sorry I'm late. I can't believe you made dinner. You shouldn't have done that."

Her brown eyes shimmered. "I wanted to."

She wanted to? Had he entered another dimension? This was Eden, the woman who'd barely dragged herself inside his house this morning, right?

"I wanted to thank you." She tilted her head to the side.

Thank him? For what? His cell phone rang. It was Chris.

He held up a finger. He'd forgotten to check the pregnant cow. His lungs tightened. *Please, let everything be all right.*

"Hey, man, I've got bad news."

"Lay it on me." Ryder retraced his steps to the mudroom.

"The pregnant red tag sixty-two?" Chris coughed.

He felt sick to his stomach. "Yeah?"

"I found her just now. The calf didn't make it."

It was his fault. All his fault. He'd let Lily's call distract him, and he'd forgotten to check on the cow. Now the calf was dead.

"That's on me, Chris. I knew I needed to check her, and I got distracted. Forgot my final round." They discussed details a few minutes before hanging up. With his throat swollen with emotion, he returned to the kitchen.

"I'm sorry to do this, but can you give me half an hour? I...I've got to go." He didn't even wait to see Eden's reaction. He jogged away, shoved his feet back into the boots, grabbed his coat and headed out into the cold wind.

He had to do better. This ranch was depending on him. The cows, the calves, the employees. Even the girls.

He couldn't make another mistake like this.

He'd make it up to Eden somehow. But for now, he had a dead calf to deal with.

Thirty minutes later, after checking on the girls contentedly watching a cartoon in the living room, Eden put their plates in the dishwasher as she listened for Ryder. The side door had slammed moments ago, and the faucet was running in the mudroom. She hoped everything was all right. The way he'd sprinted out of there earlier had her concerned.

He entered the kitchen and didn't meet her eyes.

"Thanks for…everything. I can take it from here." His subdued tone set her back.

"What's wrong?" she asked.

"Nothing." But from the look on his face, something was wrong.

"You want to talk about it?"

"There's nothing to talk about."

Okay. So they were playing that game. All day she'd wanted to extend an olive branch to him about the great job he'd done remodeling the house and for taking over the ranch, but in this instant, her goodwill fled.

"Got it." She grabbed her bag and purse and headed to the front hall. "Goodbye, girls. I'll see you tomorrow."

The twins ran to her and hugged her.

"You promise you'll be back tomorrow?" Ivy clutched Eden's hand in her own. Worry darkened her eyes.

"Of course I will, silly. I have lots of fun things planned." Eden kissed the top of her head. Then she kissed the top of Harper's. "You two get some good sleep tonight, okay?"

They hugged her again and hurried back to the couch. Ryder stood a few feet away with his arms crossed over his chest and his shoulder leaning against the wall. She couldn't read his face at all.

"See you tomorrow," she said crisply and reached for the door handle.

"Eden, wait."

She turned.

"Thank you. For staying. For dinner." His demeanor made her think he wanted to say more, but he didn't.

"You're welcome." Oddly disappointed, she opened the door and left. The wind battered her coat against her, and she braced herself all the way to her vehicle. As she let the engine warm up, she looked back at the glowing windows of the farmhouse.

Welcoming. Warm. A haven.

Her haven.

If she needed reminding that it was no longer hers and wouldn't be again, Ryder's terseness accomplished it. His less attractive qualities had come out full force, reminding her why she hadn't liked being around him until recently. They'd been getting along better, but it had only distracted her from her goals.

As much as she enjoyed spending time with the girls, she had to keep in mind that the next few months were going to fly by. And when they were over, what was she going to do?

She'd put off long-term planning. But tonight was as good as any to start researching her options. If she didn't, her life would be in even worse shape come September, and then where would she be?

Chapter Five

He wasn't the outsider looking in anymore.

Ryder had invited everyone over for pizza tonight. He stood with Mason, Dylan and local rancher Judd Wilson in his living room Friday evening. Eden, Gabby, Brittany and Nicole Taylor chatted and took care of Phoebe and the triplets in the family room. Harper, Ivy and Noah were upstairs singing at the tops of their lungs. Ryder hoped there would be many more gatherings with his new friends.

When he and Mason first met, he'd learned about Mason's support group with Gabby, Eden and Nicole. It had made him long to have a support group, too. People he could share his problems with and who would pray for him. Their group no longer formally met, but they were all still very close.

"The storm earlier this week did a number on a few of my calves. I hope yours are all right." Judd gestured to Ryder and Mason. "I'm ready for the weather to get warm again."

Mason blew out a loud breath. "It was touch and go for two of my pregnant cows, but they all made it out alive, and for that I'm grateful."

"I lost another calf this week." Ryder had spent almost a decade confident in his abilities in the financial world. But ranching? Not so much. He doubted himself on a daily basis. "The first one was my fault. I should have checked on the mother, and I... I got distracted. The second one was stillborn."

"Don't beat yourself up." Judd's eyebrows drew together as he nodded. "It comes with the territory."

"Yeah, I had no experience when I moved here last summer," Dylan said. "If it wasn't for my boss, I wouldn't have any idea what to do with the cattle. Just keep praying."

"I'm trying." Ryder didn't need to hide his mistakes. These guys weren't judging him. And he did pray every night for the Lord's guidance with the ranch. "How's married life treating you, by the way, Dylan?"

"Good. Real good." Dylan grinned. "Gabby makes life special. And Phoebe gets cuter every day. She calls me *dada* now."

"I think I'm ready for another one." Mason puffed out his chest. "It's been too long since I've been called dada."

Ryder was surprised, but then again, he shouldn't be. It was natural for Mason to want more children now that he'd remarried.

"I don't blame you. I can't wait for Phoebe to have a little sister or brother." Dylan then turned to Judd. "Have you and Nicole set a date?"

"We're working on it. Something simple. July, maybe," Judd said. "Her hands are pretty full at the moment."

They all turned to look through the archway at the women. Eden was playing patty-cake with Phoebe on her lap, and Brittany, Gabby and Nicole each held a triplet. Those babies looked good in their arms. For the first time, Ryder realized he might want another child, too.

Another baby? That wasn't going to happen.

Eden looked up just then and met his eyes. A flash

of heat spread from his head to his toes. They'd been civil to each other all week. Hadn't spent much time together or anything, and he'd been careful to come home on time each day. The twins were happy. That was the important thing.

Staring into Eden's soulful brown eyes left a yearning inside, though, similar to the one he'd experienced seeing those triplets just now. She broke eye contact first and returned her attention to Phoebe. The chubby toddler with dark curls squealed in delight.

Eden would make a terrific mother.

He gulped.

Nope. Wasn't going there.

He had no doubt Eden would eventually marry and have children of her own. But he wouldn't be involved. Couldn't be. He'd already gotten burned once, and frankly, his girls continued to get the short end of the stick from their mother. He hadn't heard from Lily since their conversation on Monday. No flight plans or dates had been set for a visit.

He'd made the right decision to not tell the girls she planned on coming. The woman changed her mind for the hollowest reasons without thinking how it would affect her daughters or him.

There had been a time when he'd thought Lily would be a terrific mother. She'd convinced him she wanted children and that her only dream was to be a stay-at-home mom. He'd told her if she wanted a career, it was fine with him. But she'd insisted she wanted to stay home. Then, after giving birth to the twins, Lily had gone behind his back and hired a nanny. She'd started auditioning again. He'd been the last to know.

She'd ignored the babies to focus on her career. She'd landed the lead in a highly anticipated movie. It had taken her away for months. She'd accepted roles on more projects until everything came to a head on the day of the twins' third birthday. He'd planned a big party for them, and that morning, Lily had pulled him aside and told him she wanted a divorce. She'd not only fallen in love with her director, but she was moving in with the guy.

She hadn't even stuck around for the girls' party.

His life had never been the same.

It had been a little over two years now, and he was still dealing with the fallout. He'd always be dealing with it. If he would have opened his eyes to acknowledge what was happening, he wouldn't have been so blindsided by Lily's betrayal.

"Ryder?" Mason asked.

He shook his thoughts back to now. "Yes?"

Laughing, Mason clapped his hand on his shoulder. "We boring you?"

"No, no. Sorry. What were you saying?"

"We're discussing moving the cattle to their summer pastures."

"Oh, right." Another thing he knew little about. "Tell me all your secrets."

"Secrets?" Mason chuckled. "There's not much to tell."

"I wait until the grass is coming in good," Judd said. "Toward the end of May is about right. Early June is fine, too."

They continued the discussion until the women came and joined them.

"It's about time I took these three home." Nicole held Amelia, the lone girl triplet, as she smiled at Judd.

"No problem." Judd nodded, taking the baby from her. Amelia yawned and wrapped her chubby arms around his neck.

"Yeah, we'd better take off, too," Dylan said to Gabby.

"I'd better get Noah." Mason moved toward the staircase, but Ryder stopped him.

"Noah can spend the night here if you want. We love having him around."

"I appreciate it, but not tonight. Brittany and I have a surprise planned for him tomorrow."

After the couples said their goodbyes, Ryder closed the door behind them and returned to the kitchen. Eden was transferring pizza slices from one box to another. He took the empty box from her hands.

"You didn't need to do that." He folded the box. He'd add it to his burn pile later. "I can clean up."

"It'll only take a minute." She blushed.

Everything about Eden was sincere. She did so many behind-the-scenes chores without expecting recognition or thanks.

Eden Page was refreshing.

Yeah, and you thought Lily was all that and a bag of chips way back when, too.

But Eden was nothing like his ex, and the evening was ending too soon for his taste. "Do you have more than a minute?"

"Why?" she asked. "Is something wrong?"

"No." He shrugged. "We haven't had much time to talk, that's all."

"What do you want to talk about?" She faced him then, blinking in confusion.

"I don't know. This house. The town. Life in Wyoming." Anything she wanted. Anything at all. "Or are you in a hurry to go home?"

"I'm not in a hurry."

"Good. Let's go to the living room. Stay for a while."

She shouldn't be staying at all, let alone for a while. Eden opened her mouth to decline, but the vulnerability in Ryder's expression stopped her. To be honest, she didn't want the night to end yet, either.

"Daddy, can we watch *Cinderella*?" Ivy asked. Her face was flushed. Harper came up behind her, yawning widely.

"Not tonight. It's past your bedtime." Ryder shook his head. "Go upstairs and get your pj's on. I'll be up in a minute to tuck you in."

"But Daddy…" both girls wailed.

"No buts. It's late."

They wore matching pouty faces and stomped out of the room.

"You." He pointed both index fingers to Eden. "Stop cleaning. Go get comfortable on the couch. I'll be back in a minute."

She suppressed a smile and wiped down the countertops while he went upstairs. She could hear him teasing the girls and their subsequent giggles. Her heart squeezed at the precious sounds. When the kitchen was clean, she dimmed the lights and went to the living room. A large sectional faced the fireplace with a massive television to the right of it. She found a spot in the corner of the sectional and reached over for a soft throw before settling it across her lap.

Yesterday Ryder had mentioned having everyone over for pizza tonight and expressly told her he wanted her there. It had meant a lot to her. So after babysitting the girls all day, she'd stayed, and it had felt good. Honestly, entertaining her friends here had felt more than good— it had felt natural. Like she was cohosting the gathering.

She frowned. She wasn't cohosting it, though. This wasn't her house. Ryder and the twins weren't her family.

Good gravy, why was she being so hard on herself? She'd spent every night this week researching going back to college. She deserved a break. It was okay to enjoy tonight. It didn't mean anything.

"Sorry about that." Ryder strode into the room and took a seat on the sectional with her. He was far enough away to not be awkward but close enough for her to be aware of him. "I give it ten minutes before they're out cold."

"We had a busy day."

"I know." He shifted, relaxing into the corner so he could face her better. "I still can't get over how much you manage to pack into your time with them."

"I love it." She did. Babysitting the twins gave her the chance to do some of the projects she'd been saving. They tucked into each task with gusto. "I've always enjoyed organizing activities and spending time with kids."

"I can tell." His eyes darkened with appreciation. The hair on her arms rose. When he looked at her like that, it was hard to concentrate. "You're making this move so much easier than I anticipated. I've been so focused on the ranch and learning about the cattle it hasn't left me nearly enough time to do the things I want to for the girls."

"Like what?"

"I promised Ivy she could have a kitten, and Harper wants to learn how to ride horses. The weather hasn't been nice enough to fully explore the ranch. I know they're going to love it. And I want to take them fishing this summer." His voice trailed off at the end as if he was getting discouraged.

"You don't have to do everything at once." Eden hadn't realized he was putting so much pressure on himself.

"I worry I won't get around to it at all." He scratched his chin. "This has been harder than I thought."

"Which part?" Ranching? Taking the girls out of California? No longer living near their mother? Adjusting to life in the country?

"Balancing cattle ranching with raising the girls."

"Ah." She nodded. "It's not easy."

His face fell. "No, it's not."

Empathy poured in. All week she'd paid attention to his interaction with Harper and Ivy. Despite the bags under his eyes and the worry lines marking his forehead, he'd grin and hug them both, asking them to show him everything they'd worked on during the day. His patience with them and the way he put their needs first had gotten under Eden's skin.

He was nothing like the man she'd thought he was before moving here.

He was better. So much better.

"When the weather gets nice," she said, "you'll be able to show the girls all the best spots on the ranch. They will love it."

"Best spots, huh?" His mouth curved into a grin that reached his eyes. "I don't know where they are."

"Oh, you will." She wrapped her arms around a throw pillow.

"You know them better than I do. I'm still getting to know the land, and I haven't seen it thawed out."

"If you follow the creek, there's a great fishing spot close to where the forest starts. We used to picnic there and fish when we were younger. The wildflowers should be blooming soon. It will take your breath away." Good memories crowded her mind of her and Mia and her parents spending afternoons by the creek.

"Perfect," he said, nodding. "Follow the creek to the forest. What else have you got?"

She thought back on all her favorite things about the ranch. There were so many. "The girls will probably want to play in the stables. Dad kept the large stall in the corner empty for us. He even installed shelves. One summer it was a toy store. Then it was a library. Sometimes we made it into a hair salon. We had a lot of fun out there."

"Your dad sounds like a great guy."

"He is." She loved her parents. Missed them now that they were traveling. They'd showered her with love as a child, and she was thankful for them every day. "Dad can come off kind of gruff, but he's a softy for kids. Oh, Mom and Mia and I used to garden, too. We canned a lot of vegetables."

"A garden." He bobbed his head side to side as if he'd never considered it. "The girls like flowers and digging and being outside. But I don't have a green thumb. I wouldn't know where to start."

"It's not overly complicated, but don't worry about it this year. You have enough to deal with." She didn't want to stare, but something in his eyes drew her in. "Ryder?"

"Yeah."

"I'm glad my parents sold the ranch to you." She meant it. He cared about it—had invested in the house, was invested in the cattle. He had a good heart. "The girls are going to be really happy here."

"Thanks, Eden. That means a lot to me."

"It's true." And it was.

"I'm not great at ranching. But I'll get there. At least, I keep telling myself I will." He ran his fingers through his hair. "I feel like my granddad's barking in my ear all day long. 'Do things right the first time. Your number-one priority is the livestock. If you lose even one sheep, you've failed.'"

"Really?" She scrunched her nose. The man sounded harsh. "Sheep die sometimes. Cattle, too. There's only so much you can control."

"I've lost two calves since taking this place over. I don't think Granddad would be too impressed."

Mason had told her that he and Ryder had been separated shortly after birth when their parents died in a car accident. Each was raised by a different set of grandparents who kept the fact they were twins a secret. She regarded Ryder. "Did you have a happy childhood?"

"Happy?" He thought about it a minute. "No, I wouldn't describe it as happy. I was taken care of, and I learned a lot of life skills, so I'm not complaining. Granddad got cancer when I was young. We sold the ranch and moved to the city to be near the hospital. He died from cancer a year later. My grandmother kind of went through the motions after he died, and she passed away my senior year of high school."

"I'm sorry, Ryder." She reached over to touch his arm. His eyes met hers, and he covered her hand with his. Then his gaze flitted to her lips, and she wondered if he thought of kissing her.

But he glanced away, and she chided herself. Why would he want to kiss her? He wasn't into her like that. They were…friends. Starting to be, at least.

"What about you?" he asked. "I know you didn't want to babysit the girls here. Has it been hard? A lot of memories of your sister?"

"Actually, it's been easy. I thought it was going to be awful. The thing is, though, the memories are still here, and I'm more at peace with her death than I've ever been. I can't really explain it."

"You don't have to."

She thought back on the years since Mia had died. All the Tuesday-night meetings with Gabby and Mason had helped her through the grief of losing her sister. Then

Nicole had joined their support group a year ago, and seeing what she'd been through had helped Eden understand that tough times happen to everyone.

Moving into the apartment, watching her parents move on, being a bridesmaid in Brittany and Mason's wedding, and now coming here, to her old home, had given her the final push she needed to move on from her sister's death.

"I hope you don't mind me inviting all your friends here tonight." He looked sheepish.

"Why would I mind? It was fun. And they're your friends, too."

"I'm glad you had fun. I, well, I envied you and Mason, Gabby and Nicole—your support group. I could have used one after Lily left me."

Ryder never discussed Lily. Eden's pulse quickened as a million questions came to mind. Why did she leave? What happened? What was it like being married to a famous star? How often did she call the girls? When was she going to visit them?

"Most of us need a support group at some point in life." She swallowed all her questions. They weren't appropriate. "I'm blessed to be best friends with them."

His eyes had that intensity again, and she wanted to look away but couldn't.

"Eden, I have a very personal question to ask, and you don't have to answer it."

Her heartbeat started pounding. "Oh, yeah?" She tried to sound nonchalant.

"Why are you still single?"

Her stomach fell to the floor. How could she possibly answer that?

I'm not pretty like Mia. I don't have the beauty, sparkling personality or talent of your ex-wife. I'm a home-

*body. Quiet. I have no idea how to flirt and don't want to,
anyhow. Guys don't notice me. I don't really blame them.*

"Never mind. It was a stupid question," he muttered.
"None of the guys around here deserve you, anyway."

Wait, what?

Did he think she'd actually turned down the single
men in Rendezvous? Was he under the impression they'd
asked her out and she'd said no? She almost laughed.

He tilted his head. "The weather is supposed to be nice
tomorrow. Why don't you come over, and we'll take the
girls on a tour of the ranch?"

She didn't know how to handle the feelings Ryder kept
bringing up. It was fine to babysit the girls. And hanging
out here when all her friends were around wasn't hurting anything. But spending additional time with Ryder?

"I don't know." She studied her hands, unwilling to
commit.

"Do you have other plans?"

"No…"

"How will I know where to take the girls if you don't
show me? I don't know how to find all these great spots
you claim are on the ranch. Come over. We'll make a
day of it."

The girls would love her favorite places on the ranch,
and the weather *was* supposed to be warm and sunny for
once. What would it hurt?

"Okay," she said. "I'll show you around."

"I'd like that." His slow grin made her gulp. "It will
be an adventure."

An adventure. Yes, the ranch was an adventure. One
she hoped would give Harper and Ivy years of fun. She'd
show them her favorite hangouts, and later, when she
wasn't part of their lives anymore, she'd rest easy knowing the ranch was being enjoyed the way it should be.

Yeah, right.

She was a hypocrite. Deep down, she wanted to spend more time getting to know Ryder. Spending it on the ranch was merely a bonus. She was playing with fire, and she knew it.

The next day, Ryder glanced over at Eden sitting in the passenger side of his truck. The girls were strapped into their booster seats in the back seat. The tires kicked up mud as they maneuvered the hills and crests of the land. Ryder had passed several places where evergreens flanked the overflowing creek. He hadn't been this way before and got excited thinking of all the acres he'd soon be able to explore.

Being out here on a sunny day made everything feel possible. Visions of fishing and riding horses and going to the twins' school events crowded his brain. They'd be happy here. He'd make sure of it.

Even Eden looked peaceful and content. She had that effect on him, too. Being around her made his problems disappear.

Rays of sun beamed on the land still recovering from winter. The grass was green and wildflowers had begun to unfurl. Maybe he'd be able to move the cattle to the summer pasture sooner rather than later.

"Once you get around the S in the creek up ahead, there will be a clearing." Eden pointed to the right. "You can stop there."

"I'm glad you know where we're going. I haven't ventured to this part of the ranch at all."

She turned to him with a smile, and he was pretty sure his heart stopped beating for a moment.

"You'll know every nook and cranny of this place soon enough."

"I hope so." He peeked at her again. "Thanks for showing us around."

"Thanks for inviting me." She returned her attention out the window.

The truck bounced over the uneven terrain, and Ryder focused on driving.

"There. See? Park up on that hill." Eden touched his arm, pointing with her other hand, and he practically jumped.

"Right." He sounded brusque.

After they parked, they all got out of the truck. Eden stretched her arms above her head. "Wow, it feels so good to be out here without wearing a coat."

Ivy and Harper held hands and ran in their new rain boots toward the creek.

"Stay away from the edge, girls," Eden called. "The water's high, and I don't want you falling in."

"Okay!" Ivy tugged Harper's hand and pointed to a clump of purple flowers growing near the trees. They bent over to inspect the blooms.

"This might be the prettiest spot in the entire state." Ryder strolled next to Eden.

"I agree." She smiled at him. "When Mia and I were young, we'd come out here in our bathing suits and lay out to get a suntan."

"Splash in the creek a little, too?"

"Yeah, a little." She laughed. "You have to be careful, though. The rocks can be sharp."

"Point taken."

"See the ridge beyond the creek?"

He squinted. "Yeah."

"If you sit up there and wait, you'll see pronghorns and mule deer and sometimes even wild horses in the distance."

"How patiently do you have to wait?" He wasn't one to sit still for long.

"It depends on the day. Bring a folding chair, a cooler and some binoculars. It's worth it."

"Maybe in ten years I'll have that kind of time." They ambled beside the creek until they reached a rocky area where the water hadn't spilled over. The girls were chasing a butterfly in the meadow.

"You need to make the time." Eden propped her foot on a boulder.

Easy for her to say. She wasn't in charge of a cattle ranch or the sole parent to twin five-year-old girls.

"Seriously, Ryder, I know what I'm talking about." Her eyebrows arched. "I'm assuming you moved here for a simpler life."

"Yeah."

"There's not much simple in this rugged land. You've got to enjoy what you can."

"Daddy, did you bring my butterfly net?" Harper ran up to him and halted, panting.

"I didn't."

"But Daddy, I *need* my net. We found a big butterfly!"

"Sorry, pumpkin. We'll bring it next time."

"C'mon, Harper." Ivy trotted up and grabbed her arm. "Let's pick flowers for Mommy."

"They'll die before she gets here, Ivy."

"No, they won't. We'll put 'em in water."

The girls took off again, but Ryder's spirits sank. "Do they mention their mother a lot while you're watching them?"

"Not all the time, but, yes, they talk about her often." Eden tilted her head. "Why?"

"I'll have to call her again," he muttered under his breath.

"I'm sure it's a big adjustment for them to not see her as often as they used to."

Not see her as often? He cocked an eyebrow. "What are you talking about?"

"Lily. Their mother." She opened her hands as if it was the most obvious thing in the world.

"What about her?"

"They miss seeing her. I'm sure this is hard on them. Being so far away from her."

"Right." He backed up, squaring his shoulders. "Lily didn't see them all that often in Los Angeles. They don't spend much time with her."

Eden frowned. "Why not?"

Because she's too busy being important. He swallowed the words. He didn't want to criticize his ex. He wouldn't. He'd learned his lesson. But he wasn't going to pretend she was something she wasn't, either. "I don't know. She didn't want to share custody, and the visitation schedules I suggest never seem to work out."

"Oh." Eden stared at the grass near her feet. "Well, the girls miss her and love her. I'm sure she'll come soon."

Eden said it like it was a good thing. He was trying to do everything in his power to help them get over the fact their mother was never around. Even when Lily did visit, she found a way to mess things up, because after she left, it took two days for him to pick up the pieces. The girls would be on cloud nine while they had her, and as soon as she left, they missed her and knew it might be months before they saw her again.

It devastated them.

And seeing them devastated always hurt him.

"Whether she comes or not doesn't change anything." He clenched his jaw. "A few days. A week. It's never enough. Our marriage—" He shook his head. "I won't make that mistake again."

"The custody arrangement?" She looked confused.

"No, marriage in general. It's not worth it."

Eden seemed to be chewing on his statement. He shouldn't have said so much.

"Daddy?" Ivy yelled. "What's this hole?"

"That hole looks like it's for a prairie dog." Eden stopped near the girls.

"A prairie dog?" Ivy shook her head. "Do they bark?"

"Kind of. They yip and make chirpy sounds." Eden chuckled. "They're not dogs at all. They're small and cute. We'll have to look up some pictures of them this week."

The girls inspected the hole for another minute, then raced off when they spotted another cluster of flowers.

"Have you given more thought to getting Ivy a kitten?" Eden asked.

Another thing he'd put on the back burner. "Not really."

"Mrs. Ball's long-haired white cat had kittens. You know Ivy has her heart set on a fluffy white cat. Want me to tell her to save one for you?"

"When would I pick it up?" He'd need to prepare. Cat litter. Food. What else did cats need?

"Oh, in a few weeks, I imagine. What about Harper?"

"What about her?"

"Do you think she'd want a kitten?"

"I don't know. Let's ask her. Hey, Harper." Up ahead, Harper turned back to him, her eyes wide and expectant. "If Ivy gets a kitten, do you want one, too?"

"I want a pony," Harper shouted.

Eden chortled. "Well, I can't help you with that."

Ivy raced to him with Harper on her heels. "Am I getting a kitty today, Daddy?"

"Not today, Ivy." He shook his head. "And Harper, no ponies. We have good horses already. I'm teaching both of you girls how to ride."

"I'm too scared, Daddy." Ivy held on to his leg, looking up at him. He ruffled her curls.

"That's exactly why I want you to learn. So you won't be scared. If you know what you're doing, horseback riding isn't scary."

"Your daddy's right, Ivy." Eden bent to her level. "It's fun when you know how."

"Are you sure, Auntie Eden?" Ivy disentangled herself from Ryder's legs to wrap her arms around Eden's neck.

"Yes."

"Okay." Turning back to Ryder, Ivy clasped her hands in front of her chest. "Can we get the kitty tomorrow?"

"No, ma'am. But we might get one in a few weeks."

"A few weeks," Ivy said breathlessly. "Did you hear that, Harper? I'm getting a kitty!"

"I still want a pony." Harper kicked at the grass. "Not a dumb old horse."

Ryder exchanged an amused glance with Eden. He'd never taught anyone how to ride horses before, and he didn't want the girls getting hurt.

"How would you feel about helping Ivy learn how to ride?" he asked Eden.

"I'm glad to be here for moral support, but if you want the girls to learn properly, talk to your brother. Mason had Noah riding pretty much from the time he could walk. You should ask him."

"Thanks, I will."

Sometimes Eden seemed too good to be true.

He'd thought Lily was everything he ever wanted, and she turned out to be a mirage. But Eden was different…

He wasn't going to throw caution to the wind now. Too much was on the line with this move. Too much could go wrong if he let his heart get too close.

Chapter Six

Two weeks later Eden stood on the corner of Third and Centennial as she waited for the Memorial Day parade to start. Brittany, Mason and Noah waved as they approached. Ever since she'd started babysitting at Ryder's place, life had been great. There was plenty of room for structured play, doing crafts and running around outside. Most evenings Eden enlisted the twins to help put together a meal. They loved tearing lettuce for a salad or putting biscuits on a plate. Ryder always invited her to stay. She usually did.

Not that she was eating supper to be near Ryder or anything. It was just lonely eating by herself in her apartment.

"Thanks for saving us a spot." Mason gave Eden a side hug, and Noah attached himself to her legs.

"Hey there, Noah-bear." Eden bent to kiss his forehead. "Are you ready for the parade?"

"I'm ready for candy." Noah wore an unzipped jacket, jeans and cowboy boots. As usual, he was bursting with energy.

Eden exchanged an amused glance with Brittany.

"He's been wound up for hours. I'm not sure candy is

a good idea." Brittany pointed to her half-zip lavender pullover, identical to Eden's. "Hey, we match."

"Sissy's Bargain Clothes?" Eden asked.

"Thirty percent off." Brittany raised her palm for a high five, and Eden slapped it. "I almost bought one for Nan, too."

"How is your grandma?"

"Slowly declining, but that's to be expected. She's still getting around okay."

"I see Ryder." Mason was craning his neck around the Johnson family, who'd squeezed in next to them. He held up his arm, and Ryder waved.

Eden hadn't realized she was holding her breath until Brittany nudged her. "Any progress on your plans?"

Plans? What plans? Seeing Ryder holding the twins' hands had erased her thought process.

"About finishing your degree." Brittany scooted closer as a couple strode by.

Oh, right. *Those* plans. Duh.

"Yeah, I'm considering it. But I don't know if early childhood education makes sense anymore. I love kids, but teaching preschool wouldn't be full-time, and I need benefits."

Brittany nodded, her blond ponytail bobbing. "I hear you. Given my job history, I'll be the first to admit they're important. Have you ever thought about teaching elementary school?"

"Not really." Eden had always been drawn to babies and toddlers, but she was enjoying Noah and the twins, too. Maybe she should consider going that route. "I'm not against it. I don't know what opportunities I'd have here in Rendezvous. The last time a teacher retired was three years ago."

"Look into it. It can't hurt." Brittany's upbeat personality always made Eden feel better.

"Thanks. I will." Whatever she did, it would be here in Rendezvous. Being an active part of Noah's life wasn't something she'd willingly turn her back on. Speaking of... Brittany and Mason had a date tonight, and Eden was looking forward to babysitting for them. "What time are you bringing Noah over?"

"Would six thirty work?"

"Perfect."

"Hey, sorry we're late." Ryder somehow created a spot next to Eden, although Bertha Johnson had staked her ground there earlier. His proximity made Eden's nerves twitch. He set the twins on the ground, then he leaned in and said, "Thanks for saving us a spot."

His warm breath near her ear was a shock. She hadn't saved him a spot—he'd shoved his way in. And she liked it. She turned her attention to the girls. "Are you excited about the parade?"

"Yes!"

"Come on, the front's where the candy's at!" Noah waved them to the curb where he stood with Mason. They wriggled through until they stood on the front lines.

"Are we all set for tomorrow?" Ryder asked Eden.

"Yes," Eden said. "Mrs. Ball has the white kitten reserved and ready for Ivy."

"Good. Last night we bought a kitty-litter box and a collar, food and a scratching post. I have no idea what else we'll need."

"It sounds like you've got the big stuff. You'll be fine. What have you done about Harper's wish?"

"Nothing." His mouth broke into a cheeky grin. "But I'm on top of it." He tapped his brother's shoulder. "Hey, Mason."

"Yeah?"

"Since the weather's nice, I'm thinking it's time to get the girls on horseback."

"Yes." Mason pumped both fists. "You are talking my language. Do you have time to buy some gear after the parade?"

"If you have time to help me."

"I've got time." Mason grinned. "Brittany? You okay with that?"

She scoffed, waving. "Go ahead. I need to stop in at the studio anyhow. Oh, there's Gabby and Dylan." Brittany beckoned them over.

"Hey, guys," Gabby said. Dylan carried Phoebe and found a spot near Mason. "I was really hoping to not have to wear a jacket today. When is it going to warm up?"

"July?" Eden teased.

"Probably." Gabby rolled her eyes, then hugged Eden and Brittany.

Nicole and Judd pushed two strollers their way. The boys were in a double umbrella stroller, and Amelia was in a single. Eden had to admit this setup appeared much more manageable than the triple stroller Nicole used to bring to church every week.

"You made it," Eden said to Nicole, then bent to greet the babies. "I hear you got into your mama's cupcake liners a few days ago, Amelia Bedelia."

"I've got to hear this," Gabby said.

"Ugh. It was the worst." Nicole bent to straighten Henry's hat. "A shipment of supplies came in, and I foolishly left the box on the floor. I turn my back for a minute, and there's Amelia tossing pink cupcake liners in the air like they're confetti."

They all laughed.

"How are you little cuties doing?" Eden covered her

eyes with her hands, then played peekaboo with the boys. Eli and Henry kicked their tiny feet and grinned at her. A familiar ache made her straighten. She loved children so much. Holding a baby was one of the greatest things in life. She'd always thought she'd hold her own someday.

She snuck a peek at Ryder, patiently listening to Harper. He didn't want marriage. And, yeah, she got along well with him, but how much of it was due to the fact she was babysitting the girls? Ninety percent? Ninety-five percent? When summer was over, he wouldn't need her anymore, and she'd be invisible Eden Page again.

Alone.

Wondering what was wrong with her.

She took in her friends, chatting, holding babies, faces glowing, and she had the sensation of being left behind. Not by them. By her circumstances.

They'd all found love. They all had families.

Was this what the rest of her life would be like? She'd be the single friend. The one secretly envying them their spouses and children. *Lord, I don't want to envy my friends. Keep me from going down that road.*

The parade kicked off with a short speech by the grand marshal followed by members of the National Guard. As high school girls dressed in fancy Western outfits and carrying flags rode horseback, Harper whirled and yelled to Ryder that she wanted a horsey and sparkly shirt, too. Eden couldn't hear his reply. She wanted to scoop the girl up and tell her of course she'd have a horse and she would buy her the sparkliest shirt in the store.

Her lungs tightened. She backed up a few steps to get some air. What was her problem?

I love these girls. She glanced at Ivy, clutching a handful of suckers and Tootsie Rolls, and Harper, bouncing around with the biggest smile. One summer with them would never be enough.

Gripping her hands together, she squeezed her eyes shut. *God, help me. I can't start wanting it again. I can't slip into the fantasy of wanting a husband and family, and I especially can't delude myself about Ryder, the girls and the ranch. I'll lose what little peace I've found.*

She'd spent the past year putting the husband, the family and the ranch off-limits. She didn't know if she could do it again. She might not have the self-control to try.

Throwing herself into finishing her degree might be the only way she could halt her growing attachment to Ryder and the girls. She'd be wise to move forward with it.

He was getting too close to Eden. The next morning in church, Ryder handed packets of fruit snacks to the girls as they waited for the service to begin. Harper sat to his right. Ivy to his left. They each had a small notebook, a sheet of stickers and a few crayons to keep them occupied.

Ivy kept poking her head around to look at the entrance. The twins had been tired this morning when he'd gotten them up. After the parade yesterday, Eden had slipped away without giving him a chance to say goodbye. He and Mason had taken the kids shopping at the Western store for riding gear, and he'd found himself wishing Eden had joined them.

"Auntie Eden's here!" Ivy whispered loudly. Kneeling on the pew, facing the entrance, she waved Eden over. As soon as Eden neared, Ivy hopped down and reached for her hand. "Sit with us."

Ryder didn't bother reprimanding her. He'd have a talk with her later about not messing around in the pew. At the moment, all he could do was fight awareness.

Eden wore a short-sleeved white shirt with a flowy coral-colored skirt and strappy sandals. Her hair spilled over her shoulders, and he caught the scent of her perfume. Clean and floral. All Eden.

She glanced at him and smiled. His mouth went dry. He'd been enjoying their time together every evening. When he came in from the ranch each weekday, he wanted to pinch himself. Eden was usually directing the girls how to set the table, where a hearty meal would be waiting.

How did she do it? How in the world did she spend so much time preparing activities for the girls, playing with them, reading to them, helping them make their books for Lily and, on top of it all, cooking supper?

He'd already slipped a bonus for her into each week's check. She'd called him out on it, of course, but he told her she earned it.

She earned every penny and more.

The opening hymn filled the air, and he scanned the bulletin to follow along. Ivy had settled on Eden's lap, and from the corner of his eye he could see Eden's fingers stroking her hair. She was so good to his girls.

Why hadn't she gotten married? A beautiful woman like her—one who loved kids, was dependable and genuine, and could cook better than most people he knew—should have gotten snatched up long ago by a local cowboy.

There he went again. Making assumptions. Maybe Eden had something against marriage. Or the right guy hadn't come along yet. He'd made assumptions with Lily, too, and look where it had gotten him.

Ryder turned his attention back to the hymn and sang along. Several minutes later, Harper yawned loudly and climbed onto his lap. He peeked at Eden. She stared straight ahead as the pastor gave the sermon. Then she kissed the top of Ivy's head and held her closer.

His heart contracted. His little girls hadn't had much maternal affection in their lives.

Stop thinking about Eden. Get your mind on the sermon.

He tried. He really did. But beyond noting the theme of God knows our needs better than we do, he didn't get much out of it. If he wasn't thinking about Eden, he was thinking about the ranch. They'd started prepping the summer pasture this week. He was getting the hang of cattle. Of course, every day or two a new problem arose that he had no idea how to deal with. Thankfully, Chris had a good head on his shoulders. And if Chris didn't know what to do, Ryder called Mason.

The congregation got to their feet, and Ryder easily hefted Harper up as he stood. Eden shifted. Ivy had fallen asleep, too, so she picked her up, and it was as if he was momentarily outside his own body. With Eden standing next to him, each holding a twin in their arms, the image appeared so right he could barely breathe.

They looked like a family. A real family. A mom, dad and their two girls.

"Let us bow our heads and pray," the pastor said.

Ryder ignored the pastor's prayer for one of his own. *God, I need some help here. I knew I was playing with fire asking Eden to babysit the girls. It doesn't help that I'm friends with all of her friends. Spending all this time together is making me feel things I don't want to feel. Will You give me strength? Help me avoid temptation?*

When the service ended, the girls rubbed their sleepy eyes. As ushers directed people out of their pews, Ivy's face lit up and she gasped. "It's kitty time, isn't it, Daddy?"

He'd almost forgotten. They were picking up the kitten right after church.

"You're coming with us, right, Auntie Eden?" Ivy's big eyes grew worried.

"Yes, I am. I can't wait to see your kitten." Eden tapped the tip of Ivy's nose. "I'm going to go to my apartment and change first, though. Okay?"

"Okay."

Another afternoon with Eden. His pulse sped up at the thought. But fear was mixed with anticipation. Nothing involving his heart was ever simple. Not even picking up a kitten.

An hour later, Ivy cradled the wiggly kitten in her arms back at the ranch. Eden had met Ryder and the girls at Mrs. Ball's house, and when Ivy spotted the white kitten reserved for her, she'd burst into happy tears, thanking her daddy over and over. Even Harper, who hadn't been enthused about getting a cat, had oohed and aahed over the remaining kittens. She'd fallen hard for a striped gray one, and in the end, Ryder had brought it home, too. Eden was helping the girls with the felines while Ryder went upstairs to change out of his church clothes.

"What are you going to name yours, Ivy? Mine looks like Scruffy or Silver or Wonderkitty. She's so soft. Maybe I should name her Dandelion, like the fluff we blow and make a wish on." Harper didn't seem to mind that her kitten had climbed onto her shoulder and was batting at her hair with one paw.

"I want a pretty name. She's like a princess. Meow. Meow." Ivy's kitten tried valiantly to escape her grip, but Ivy wasn't letting go. "Stop squirming."

In jeans and a T-shirt, Ryder jogged down the staircase. "Why don't you let the kittens explore for a while. They won't want to be held every minute."

"Good idea. Let's keep them in one spot for now." Eden pointed to the sunroom. "I'll watch them for you while you change into play clothes."

"Do I have to change?" Ivy whined, kissing her kitten's head again and again. "My kitty will miss me."

"Yes." Ryder was firm. "Cats do not want to be held all the time."

Or at all. Eden kept her thoughts to herself. Some cats loved being held. Others hated it.

"Goodbye, kitty. I'll be right back. I'm not leaving you. Promise." Ivy took hers to the sunroom and set it on the love seat. Harper did the same, then skipped out the door behind her sister.

Eden started to shut the French door, but Ryder blocked it with his foot.

"You trying to get rid of me or something?" His eyes gleamed in amusement as he slipped into the room, closing the door behind him. "Thanks for setting us up with the kittens. They are a hit."

"You're welcome. I'm glad you got Harper one, too. It's easier to deal with young littermates than introducing another cat later on." Eden thought back to when Mia had found a cat on the side of the road and brought it home. Their older cat, Brownie, had not been happy. There had been a few days of hissing before the two could tolerate being in the same room.

Eden scooped up the striped kitten and sat on the love seat with it. It immediately began to purr. The little rumbles cheered her heart. "This one is so cute. I'm tempted to go back and get the last kitten for myself."

"Why don't you?" He plunked his body down on an

oversized chair. Ivy's kitten crawled between his chair and the wall.

"I don't know. Where would I put the litter? I don't even know what my plans are after the summer. It wouldn't be fair to the poor little thing." The kitten launched itself off her lap onto the floor and chased its sister.

Ryder scooched forward. "What do you mean? What's happening after the summer? You're not moving, are you?"

"No, definitely not. I would never leave Noah. I promised Mia I'd always be part of his life. I want to be here to spend time with him and watch his sports and school plays. I love him so much."

He nodded, his face clearing. "Then what's the deal with this fall?"

"I'm at a crossroads." Somehow over the past month, she'd gotten comfortable being with him. She wanted to open up to him. "When I found out Mia had cancer, it was the first semester of my junior year of college. I finished the term and moved back home. Noah was only six months old when my sister died, and Mason couldn't take care of the baby and the ranch, so I became Noah's full-time babysitter. It saved me."

"Saved you?" He eased back, crossing one leg and resting his ankle on his knee. "What do you mean?"

"Losing my sister so young was something I never could have imagined. It was unbelievable. Indescribable. I had a hard time accepting it. Taking care of her baby gave me a purpose. I'm very thankful for that time."

"Didn't you want to go back to college?"

"No."

Harper's kitten saw a leaf blowing outside and jumped

onto the other chair in front of the window. Its little tail swished back and forth quickly.

"You babysat him until Mason and Brittany got married, right?"

"Yeah. And by then I was babysitting Phoebe, too." She picked a piece of lint off the cushion next to her. "But a lot has changed in five years. Everyone's moving on, and I need to, too. I'm thinking of finishing my degree online. I originally went to school for early childhood education, but I'm looking at other majors. I need benefits."

"What are you going to do instead?"

"I don't know. Maybe I'll be an elementary school teacher."

"You'd be terrific at it."

"You think?" His compliment planted seeds of hope in her heart.

"Look at how great you are with the girls. The activities you plan, the books you read to them, the projects you've been preparing for their mother. I can't thank you enough."

"Have you heard from Lily? Does she plan on visiting soon?" Eden was surprised their mother hadn't come out yet. The girls were so enthusiastic whenever they added pages to their books.

"I don't know."

"I'm having a hard time putting them off." Eden didn't want to make him feel bad, but it was true. "They talk about her a lot."

"I know." He tapped his thumb against his leg. "It would make it easier on all of us if she would visit."

Eden was taken aback. She'd assumed he didn't want Lily to visit, especially after his cryptic words about marriage being a mistake. She'd been pounding it in her head every time the urge hit to think of him as more than a friend.

"Maybe you could ask her," she said softly.

"I have." His eyes were bleak. He shifted his jaw. "I'll keep trying."

He had asked her. Why had she assumed he hadn't?

"I never imagined an entire month would go by without her seeing them," Eden said almost to herself.

"It's been longer than a month." He lifted one shoulder in a careless shrug, but Eden wasn't fooled. It bothered him. "She was on location for their birthday, so I guess it would have been around Christmas since they last saw her."

"Is that normal?" It couldn't be right. Surely Lily spent more time with them than that. There had to be an explanation. "Was she shooting a movie or series or something?"

"She's not always great about following through with plans. She'll tell them she's coming to see them, and at the last minute, she'll back out, or worse, not show up at all."

Eden tried to wrap her head around this new information.

"Before you defend her—" he raised his hands "—I'm not trying to bad-mouth her. She's not an awful person. Trust me, I want the girls to have a mother. I do what I can, but…"

Eden wasn't sure what to think. Maybe Lily was really busy or felt uncomfortable with Ryder or something.

"I've told her over and over she can take them for a weekend or go to Disneyland with them, whatever." Ryder turned his attention out the window. "For a while, I worried she was trying to avoid me and that's why she wasn't showing up. But she wasn't around much even when we were married."

Well, there went that theory.

"Where's my kitty?" Ivy opened the door and ran inside with her arms wide-open, fingers curling in and out. Harper wasn't far behind. The white kitten poked its head out from under Ryder's chair. "Daddy! You're not s'posed to let her get dirty!"

His expression softened. Harper bounced over to the striped cat rolling on the area rug. "My kitty can do whatever she wants. If she feels like jumping in a mud puddle, I'm gonna let her."

"She better not get *my* kitten all muddy." Ivy got down on her knees and dragged the white kitten out from under the chair. Carefully holding her the way Mrs. Ball demonstrated, Ivy proceeded to scold the cat. "You're not a dust mop. Now go lick your fur and get clean." The kitten wiggled to be set down, and Ivy lost her grip. It pounced on Harper's, and they rolled around, playing.

"Can we call Mommy?" Ivy set her hands on Ryder's knees and gazed at him. "I want her to help me name my kitty."

Eden held her breath as she watched Ryder for his reaction. Would he approve?

"I'll call her now." His tender smile for Ivy sent a wave of warmth through Eden's core.

He hadn't shot down his daughter's desire to talk to her mommy.

An uncomfortable feeling tugged at her conscience. Why did she keep assuming the worst about him? And why did she keep giving his ex-wife the benefit of the doubt?

Eden had never even met her.

Maybe it was time to face facts. Shortly after meeting Ryder, Eden had taken sides—Lily's—without ever having met her.

And now that she knew Ryder, she could admit he wasn't an inconsiderate jerk who kept his daughters from their mother. He was a hardworking man doing the best he could to make a nice life for them.

The bricks she kept trying to pile up against him were toppling down one by one. She wasn't sure how to keep propping them up anymore.

All she knew was if she didn't, she'd be in trouble. Because the man in front of her wasn't the ogre she needed him to be.

Chapter Seven

"That's going to be a problem."

Wednesday afternoon, Ryder looked ahead to where Chris pointed. They were checking the fence surrounding the first section of summer pasture in preparation for moving the herd. Strands of barbed wire had gone slack near the bottom of one of the fence posts. Ryder dismounted. After hammering it to secure it, he turned back to inspect the wire. Looked good.

"Good eye, Chris." Ryder got back in the saddle, and they continued on. They still had miles of fence to inspect. They couldn't have asked for a better day to do it. The first week of June had brought mild temperatures, a breeze and sunshine. He wished every day could be this pleasant.

"I've had a lot of practice." A thin man in his late thirties with a scruffy brown beard, Chris had a body as tough as beef jerky. He seemed tense. Normally, he chatted about the ranch, cattle, his son or the upcoming rodeo season. Today he'd been quiet.

"Something on your mind?" Ryder pulled up alongside him.

"Just making sure we have this pasture locked down.

The cows have a knack for finding the weakness in a fence and waving all their girlfriends through."

Ryder had seen it firsthand himself. "You're not wrong."

"They must be related to my ex," Chris muttered.

"She giving you problems?" Every once in a while, Chris would comment on how unreasonable his ex-wife was about their custody arrangement, but most days the man didn't say much on the topic.

"When doesn't she? She knows my weaknesses and uses them against me, too, just like the cows." Chris continued to scan the fence as they rode through thick green grass. "I was supposed to take Trevor to the rodeo Friday night, but now she's claiming they have some family event to attend. This is the fifth time this year she's done this. If it's not a cousin's birthday, it's a surprise party for her parents' wedding anniversary. I get every other weekend with Trevor, starting Friday afternoon, and I'm mighty tired of giving up my days for her family."

Ryder could see his point. "Can you switch dates with her?"

"I have. Half the time, she finds an excuse to keep him on the days we switched, too. I'm tired of it. I've told Trevor time and again we would be going to the rodeos all summer long. They're on Friday nights. If she takes my Fridays, I can't keep my word to my son." Chris shook his head. "Women aren't worth it. They trick you into thinking they're sweet and nice, and then—bam! They mess you up."

Uneasiness stirred in Ryder's gut. What Chris was describing had been his own experience, too. Lily had been sweet and nice when they'd met. He hadn't been able to believe his good fortune when the amazing, gorgeous, and very famous actress noticed him. They'd had a whirlwind romance, and he'd been smitten.

"I'm not giving in this time," Chris said. "She'll throw a hissy fit, but I don't care. Smartest thing I ever did was go through the courts to nail down a custody arrangement. I'm picking up my son this Friday no matter what she says. She'll hear from my lawyer if she gets in my way."

"How does your son feel about it?" Ryder thought of Ivy and Harper and the hope shining on their sweet faces every time they thought their mother would call or visit. How many times had their hopes been crushed? Too many to count. Just look at Sunday when he'd left message after message for Lily to call the girls. They'd been so excited to tell her about their kittens. He'd yet to hear back from her.

"I don't know." Chris glanced his way and blew out a frustrated breath. "Stuck in the middle, I suppose."

Ryder could relate. He often felt stuck in the middle between Lily and the girls. It made him feel helpless.

He couldn't force Lily to care about their daughters' feelings.

He couldn't force her to show up.

"Working here has been a lifesaver." Chris's hazel eyes sharpened as he stared at Ryder. "Rendezvous is close enough for me to be around my son, but far enough away to not be under her family's judgmental eye. I had to get out of that town."

"You've been a lifesaver for me, too." They continued to ride along the fence. "Mason gave me a crash course in ranching on the weekends I could get here, but riding out with you every day is what's really gotten me up to speed."

"You took to it quickly," Chris said. "Do me a favor,

boss. If I ever start talking about dating again, give me a swift boot in the backside, okay?"

Ryder laughed. "Will do." He almost asked Chris to do the same for him, but Eden's face came to mind. *Sweet and nice.* Unlike Lily, Eden *was* sweet and nice. But like Lily, she had goals and dreams that didn't involve him, like getting her degree. She'd already set aside her college plans once. He didn't want her to set them aside again.

He saw how she was with the girls—devoted, loving, selfless. Having her around made life so much easier for him. But it didn't mean he could pursue anything with her.

When was the last time life had been this smooth? *When Lily was pregnant with the twins...*

They'd hired a decorator to help design the babies' rooms, taken child-birthing classes, gone out to restaurants, laughed a lot and picked out names. Lily had wrapped up the final season of *Courtroom Crimes* before they got married and was on a hiatus. They'd decided to start their family right away. That year—the marriage, the pregnancy—had a surreal quality to it. Everything had been like a dream come true.

Then the twins came. Two beautiful, squawking, healthy girls. Ryder had never felt so much sheer love in his life. Within days, Lily scrapped the idea of being a homemaker, and she hired a nanny. He understood. Two babies were a lot.

But then things changed, and he'd been trying to keep his head above water ever since.

"Looks like we've got another section down." Chris slowed where wire dangled between posts. "It's a good thing we're checking this before we move the herd in. Nothing worse than having to track down cattle when we could be getting other work done. This will prevent a lot of problems later on."

Truer words had not been spoken. Remembering how Lily played him for a fool, how she'd lied to him and acted like the twins were disposable would prevent a lot of problems for Ryder, too.

He didn't think he was capable of trusting a woman again the way he'd trusted Lily. He was not getting sucked into a relationship where the woman he loved claimed to want one thing but really wanted something else entirely. Something that didn't involve him.

Repairing this fence would keep the cattle in. Repairing the fence around his heart would keep complicated feelings out.

"I want twisty ice cream with sprinkles!" Harper held on to the edge of the counter at Dipping Dream's takeout window.

"I want chocolate with sprinkles," Ivy said.

Eden hiked Phoebe higher on her hip. They'd just loaded up on books from the library and had walked the two blocks to the ice-cream stand. Harper had skipped the entire way here, while Ivy held Eden's hand and walked beside her.

Sunday afternoon, she'd made a to-do list involving ordering her transcripts, setting up a phone call with an adviser and printing out the current requirements to get certified as a teacher in Wyoming. Then, yesterday, while the girls watched a video, she'd called the local elementary principal. Eden had been pleasantly surprised to find out she could do her student teaching there when the time came, and later she could substitute teach as a gateway to full-time employment.

Phoebe reached a chubby hand toward Harper's hair.

"Oh, no, you don't." Eden stopped her from grabbing a fistful of waves. "I'm getting you ice cream, too, Phoebe-kins."

"Cwee," Phoebe said, her eyes lighting up.

"Yep."

"What can I get for you?" the teen behind the window asked.

Eden sensed Phoebe getting ready to go for Harper's hair again, so she shifted out of reach. "We'll take one twisty cone with sprinkles, one chocolate cone with sprinkles, one vanilla cup and a hot fudge sundae."

"Coming right up." He disappeared from view.

Eden scanned the area for places to sit. A picnic table nearby was free. "Why don't you girls sit at that table while I wait for the ice cream?"

She watched as they raced over and sat opposite each other. Shifting shadows from the tree nearby partially shaded it. An employee held two cones with sprinkles out the window. Now what? She had only one hand free.

"I'll be right back for the other one." Eden carefully took the twisty cone to the table, where, to her surprise, Misty Sandpiper was taking a seat.

Harper sat on her knees, leaning in to hear Misty better, and Ivy's gaze was glued her face. Eden wasn't exactly friends with Misty. She didn't dislike her or anything, but they ran in different circles.

Misty was outgoing and popular and always had a boyfriend. In other words, the exact opposite of Eden.

"Want me to hold Phoebe for you?" Misty always looked put together and pretty in a natural way with her long light brown hair and carefully applied makeup. She was wearing denim shorts with a low-cut hot-pink T-shirt.

"Thank you, that would be great." Eden handed

Phoebe to her and hurried back to get the rest of the ice cream. It took two trips, but finally, she was able to sit next to Harper. Then she realized she'd stuck Misty with the baby. "Oh, what am I thinking? Here, I'll take Phoebe."

"I don't mind feeding her." She made cute faces at Phoebe, who extended both hands toward the cup of vanilla with her mouth wide-open.

"Are you sure?" When Misty nodded, Eden rummaged through the diaper bag. "I'll get her bib. She can be messy."

She handed it to Misty, who snapped it over Phoebe's T-shirt. The sprinkles were already starting to fall off the sides where the ice cream dripped from the twins' cones.

"Girls," Eden said, "lick those drips before they fall onto your hands. Here are some napkins." She pushed a few napkins to them.

"What brings you out today?" Eden asked, keeping an eye on each of her charges. Harper had licked one side of her cone, but sprinkles freely dripped onto the back of her hand. Ivy was valiantly circling hers, but it was dripping nonetheless. And Phoebe was smiling and clapping every time Misty gave her another bite from her cup of vanilla ice cream.

"I have the day off," Misty said. "I'd just finished my shake when I saw these two sit down."

"We got kitties," Harper said. An ice-cream mustache crested her lip. "Mine is silver and has stripes like a tiger."

"What did you name him?" Misty directed her attention to Harper. Phoebe tried to grab the spoon and held her mouth open for another bite. Misty fed her a spoonful of vanilla.

"She's a girl. Her name's Dandy. It's short for Dandelion, cuz she's so fluffy. Do you ride ponies? I started to learn. My uncle Mason's teaching me. Daddy's helping Ivy cuz she's scared." Harper took another long lick.

"Am not!" Ivy furrowed her eyebrows. "I rode Nugget. Daddy told me I did good."

"Well, Uncle Mason says I'm real good at it. Patches can tell."

"Stop bragging, Harper."

This type of back-and-forth happened several times a day, so Eden quickly changed topics. "Why don't you tell Misty what you named your kitten, Ivy?"

"Princess Cutie." Ivy took another lick from her cone. "She's white and fluffy and she purrs all the time. I just call her Cutie. It's easier that way. And she sure is cute."

Harper jumped in. "I have a sparkly shirt to wear when I ride Patches. Do you have sparkly shirts when you ride a horse? Mine's purple and white. I like the baby-blue one I saw in the store, too. Have you seen it?" Harper's ice cream was beginning to melt down the back of her hand. "Auntie Eden, it's a river!"

Eden sopped up the mess with the napkins she had on hand.

"Cwee, cwee!" Phoebe yelled, slapping her palms on the picnic table.

Misty's eyes had the overwhelmed expression Eden often felt when dealing with three young girls. She reached over for the baby. "Let me take her."

Misty transferred her to Eden and pushed the ice-cream cup her way, then turned to Harper once more. "I used to have a lot of sparkly outfits. In fact, I competed in rodeos."

"Rodeos," Harper said reverently. "I want to ride in one."

"Not me." Ivy licked the drips around her cone.

"That's cuz you're scared."

"Am not!"

"Girls." Eden tried to keep her voice even. "Let's be nice."

"I was scared of riding when I was younger," Misty said. "My mama got so mad at me. She said no self-respecting Wyoming girl didn't know how to ride a horse."

"What did you do?" Ivy watched Misty above her cone.

"First, I cried a little. I thought she was so mean. Then I toughened up. My daddy took me out and told me he'd be right there next to me and not to worry. So I didn't."

"My daddy told me the same." Ivy nodded.

"You've got a good daddy." Misty smiled. "He won't let you fall. I wouldn't mind coming out to help if you want."

Great. Now Misty would be at the ranch, and Ryder would be dazzled by her bubbly personality and pretty face. Eden spooned the last bite of ice cream into Phoebe's mouth. "I need to clean her up."

"I'll stay here with the girls."

"You don't mind?"

"Not at all."

"Thanks."

Eden grabbed the diaper bag and took Phoebe to the public restroom at the side of the ice-cream stand. The mirror showed white smears on the shoulder of her shirt where Phoebe had placed her sticky hands. Eden's hair was frizzing near her face, and strands of hair had escaped her ponytail. Needless to say, the swipe of tinted lip gloss she'd applied this morning had worn off hours ago.

Misty always looked impossibly fresh and nice. No wonder she always had a date while Eden sat home. And

Eden couldn't even hate the girl. She'd been really nice and helpful today.

She wet a paper towel and washed Phoebe's hands and face with it as the child did everything in her power to avoid getting wiped. In the end, Phoebe let out a few high-pitched shrieks before Eden was confident she'd eliminated all the stickiness.

Back outside, her stomach dropped at the sight of Ivy and Harper hanging on Misty's words and laughing at something she said. Eden had been around Rendezvous enough to see the writing on the wall. She'd had Ryder to herself since he'd moved to town, but that would be changing.

She didn't want Ryder to fall for pretty, flirty Misty Sandpiper. She wanted him to fall for her.

And that wasn't going to happen.

Friday afternoon, Ryder took a seat in the ranch office and glanced at the whiteboard listing all the projects he needed to get done this summer. The day was warm and sunny. He and Chris had started moving the cattle to their new pasture. Everything was going well for the moment. The kittens had distracted Ivy from her constant questions about when her mother was coming, and Harper hadn't stopped begging to ride Patches again. Both girls were getting another horseback-riding lesson tomorrow when Mason was free to help him.

His cell phone rang, and he glanced at it. Lily's name appeared. A copper taste coated his tongue.

"What's up?" He kept his tone friendly, crisp.

"Hi, Ryder." Her silky voice slid through the line. "How are the girls?"

"They're fantastic." His grip on the phone tightened.

It was on the tip of his tongue to tell her she'd know how they were if she'd ever get around to seeing them.

"Good. I have a break in my schedule. I'm making arrangements to visit."

He'd believe it when she appeared on his doorstep. Not one second sooner.

"Good." He drummed his fingertips on the desk. "My offer still stands if you want to stay here at the ranch."

"I've actually had Mandy rent a cabin for me."

A cabin implied rustic. What she really meant was she'd rented a luxury log home. But what did he care? Cabin, mansion—at least she was coming.

Maybe.

"When do you arrive?"

"Next Friday. I plan on staying a week."

That gave him a week to get ready. No problem. "They will be very happy. They want to see you. By the way, I bought them kittens. Maybe you could FaceTime the girls later so they can show them to you. And you can let them know you're coming."

"Yes, absolutely," she said brightly. "Oh, gotta run. I'll have Mandy send you the information." And she hung up.

He stared at the phone in his hand and shook his head. Would she keep her word? And if she did come, would she spend an entire week with the girls?

He wasn't counting on it. Couldn't count on her. Maybe he could ask Eden to be on call that week. Leaning back, he sighed.

Harper's and Ivy's faces came to mind with all their innocent questions about their mother coming to see them.

Lily had better not let them down this time.

At least if she didn't show up, Eden would be around to help him pick up the pieces.

But what would he do when summer ended? He'd be on his own again, doing his best to raise the twins by himself. They needed their mother, too, and he couldn't force her to be involved in their lives.

He wouldn't think about it now. He had a ranch to run.

"No, Dandy, don't hide under there." Harper crouched down on all fours and peeked under the couch. Then she scrambled to her feet. "Auntie Eden, Dandy doesn't like me!"

Eden calmly went over to where Harper stood. "What's the problem?"

"She's under the couch, and I told her not to. Bad kitty!" Harper stamped her little bare foot on the hardwood floor and pouted.

"Cutie is being bad, too." Ivy carried the wiggly kitten over from where she'd plucked her off the curtains. "Her claw scratched me, and Daddy said she can't climb the curtains."

"Why don't you both leave the kittens alone for a while, and we'll have some cookies outside. Your daddy will be home soon."

Late afternoon could be cagey with the twins, even on a beautiful, sunny summer Friday. At least Phoebe had been happy all day. Gabby had picked her up an hour ago, leaving Eden alone with the twins.

"Okay." Ivy set the kitten on the couch, but it promptly leaped off and raced to the curtains. "Auntie Eden! She's doing it again!"

"Let's put the kitties in a time-out in the sunroom." Eden reached under the couch and moved her arm until she got a grip on Dandy. Then, holding the kitten, she hustled over to the curtains and plucked Cutie off. After depositing the furballs in the sunroom and shutting the door, she headed back down the hall, where she could hear the girls bickering in the family room.

"No, I get to tell Mommy about the kitties first." Ivy jabbed her thumb into her chest.

"Fine. We never talk to her anyhow." Harper sounded mad. "Who cares?"

"Don't say that about Mommy." Ivy's voice went up an octave. "She's busy. Daddy said so."

"Phoebe's mommy isn't too busy for her," Harper said.

"Maybe Mommy doesn't know where Wyoming is. I told Daddy she couldn't find us."

"She can use her phone like Daddy does when he gets lost." Harper's face fell. "She doesn't love us."

"She loves us." Ivy didn't sound so sure.

Eden's heart fell to the floor. She'd better go in there before the girls argued themselves into a puddle of hurt they couldn't get out of.

"Don't cry," Harper said. Eden paused at the end of the hall and watched them. Harper wrapped her arms around Ivy. "You're right. She loves us. She does."

Eden didn't know what to do. What could she say? She didn't know how to handle this situation. Retracing her steps to the kitchen, she selected a package of cookies. They probably weren't the healthy solution, but the girls needed a distraction at the moment.

"Ready, girls?" She pasted on a bright smile. "We'll have a snack outside. Grab a blanket."

Eden slid open the patio door and followed them to the grass where they spread out the blanket. She knelt on it and took out the cookies. The girls joined her. After a few minutes of munching, they all sprawled out and played several rounds of I spy.

"I spy with my little eye…" Harper chanted. "Daddy!"

"Hey there, Harper." Ryder stopped at the edge of the blanket. "Ivy. Eden."

"We didn't hear you coming." Her breath caught at how rugged he looked in his T-shirt and jeans. His face had a carefree expression she wasn't used to seeing.

"This looks fun. Is there room for me?" He crouched with his elbows on his knees.

"Yes, Daddy, right here." Ivy patted the spot between her and Eden. He raised his eyebrows and squeezed into the spot.

Eden should have moved aside. She still could. But she didn't want to.

Ryder was all cowboy. Sitting next to him was sweeter than the chocolate sandwich cookies she'd just devoured.

"You know what day it is?" he asked the girls.

"Friday!" They hopped to their feet. "Pizza day!"

"Yep. Why don't you go inside and get washed up? I'll be in there in a minute."

"Okay!" They ran inside, leaving Eden all too aware she was alone with their very handsome daddy.

"Want to join us? Roscoe's makes a mean meat-lover's." His eyes gleamed with appreciation and more.

Did she want to join them? Of course she did. She loved being with the girls, enjoyed eating supper with the three of them.

But caution held her back. Maybe it was seeing Misty the other day or the fact she'd spoken with an academic adviser and was 99 percent sure she was enrolling in on-line classes this fall. Regardless, she needed to face facts.

She'd been getting too wrapped up in this family.

"No, I can't. I have plans." She *did* have plans, too. Mason had asked her to babysit Noah tonight.

"Oh." His face fell. "Too bad. While I've got you here, I figure I'd better mention Lily called earlier. As of right now she plans on flying in next Friday and spending a week with the girls."

Eden tried to keep her face from crumbling. Wasn't this what she wanted? Why did it feel like the beginning of the end? "That's great. The girls really miss her. It will do them a world of good to see their mom."

"Yeah, well…" He shrugged. "She's not always reliable."

"You mentioned that." Eden treaded carefully. "They were upset earlier. They argued about her. Spending time with their mom will help."

"She said she'll FaceTime them tonight." He cocked his head as if he didn't believe it. "She told me the same thing last week, and it never happened."

"I'm sure her job has a lot of pressures." Even so, Eden couldn't imagine not talking to Harper and Ivy if they were hers.

"It does." He turned to stare at her. "I hope she keeps her word. Can you still be available to babysit in case she changes her mind about coming? I'll pay you no matter what. In fact, I might need you to be on call."

"Of course." She wanted to be there for Ivy and Harper. And Ryder. "It's not a problem."

"Thank you." Appreciation and more shimmered through his eyes. "About the girls being upset…maybe I should talk to them."

"Please don't. They didn't know I heard them."

"I have a feeling I don't know half of what they're going through. I wish…" He shook his head. "Never mind. Some mistakes can't be undone."

She frowned. "What do you mean?"

"I wish I could have done it all differently. I want better for them. Their mother has incredible gifts. She can be the life of the party, the most understanding friend."

Eden's heart bottomed out with each word.

"But it's temporary. It doesn't last. If she had any idea how much the twins look up to her and want her to be in their lives, she'd…" Once more he shook his head.

The girls came back out as his ringtone sounded. "Speaking of Lily. I have a FaceTime coming in. Do you mind?" He stared at Eden.

"Not at all." She stood. "I'll show myself out."

"Mommy!" Ivy screeched as Ryder answered the call.

As Eden walked toward the house, she heard Lily's soothing, upbeat voice and the girls tripping over each other's words in an effort to speak. She trudged inside, packed her supplies, straightened the art projects and let herself out the front door.

She was only the babysitter. Ryder had been clear he considered marriage a mistake. And he was right that if Lily had any idea how much the twins looked up to her, she'd make more effort with them.

Sometimes the hardest things to do were the right ones. If Lily was coming next week, Eden would do her best to show the woman what amazing little girls she had. And in the meantime, she needed to limit her own time with their daddy.

She was in no shape to fall for Ryder Fanning, and if she didn't keep reminding herself, she'd tumble over the cliff and never recover.

Chapter Eight

"Surprise!" Eden's mom and dad stood in the doorway of her apartment the next morning. She'd just showered and brewed a pot of coffee. Her parents hadn't planned on coming back to town until next month, so this was a happy development. Dad looked like he'd put on ten pounds since leaving the ranch, and Mom was as beautiful as ever with her gray eyes and shoulder-length dark brown hair.

"When did you get here?" After ushering them inside, Eden hugged them both. "Why didn't you call?"

"We wanted to see the look on your face when we arrived." Her dad winked at her. "How are you doing, kid?"

"I'm good, Dad." She pointed them to the living room and detoured into the kitchen. "Coffee's ready if you want some."

"I'll take a cup," her mother called. "Cream and sugar, please."

"Black for me." Dad followed her to the kitchen and reached into an upper cabinet for a mug. He selected a big one with a sketch of a bull. "Ah, you still have my favorite."

"It reminds me of you." Eden laughed. She prepared

a mug of coffee for her mom as Dad poured his own. "How was Tennessee?"

Together, they headed to the living room.

"The Smoky Mountains were something. But it's good to be back where you can see miles of land without so much civilization getting in the way."

"We've met so many people." Mom accepted the mug from Eden with a smile. Eden sat on one of the chairs adjacent to the couch. "I never imagined how different each state could be."

"Different in some ways, but the same in others." Dad took a seat opposite Eden. "There's a McDonald's everywhere you turn. Same stores, same highways. And a lot of traffic." He pretended to shudder.

"Sounds like you're missing Wyoming, Dad." Eden studied him. Aside from his not-too-serious aversion to civilization, he looked more carefree than he had in years. Retirement seemed to be suiting him.

"Yeah, I guess I am." His wistful expression ended with a slight shrug. "Don't get me wrong. I'm enjoying seeing new places."

"I know." She was glad her parents were doing something that made them happy. Still, it came as no shock to her that her dad might be missing home. "Do you want to stay here while you're in town? I can get the air mattress out."

"Oh, no." Mom waved her off. "We're set up at Rendezvous Pines campground. The spacious campsites are a welcome change from some of the tiny lots where we've parked."

"How's Ryder doing with the ranch?" Dad's knee bounced as he watched her.

"Fine, I guess."

"The herd? He's doing okay with the cattle?"

"Yep. Same as I told you last week." She regularly talked to her parents, and her dad always asked about the ranch. "I think they moved cattle this week."

"Good. Good." Dad took a drink of his coffee. "Did he check all the fence? Get the calves branded?"

"Yes, he did." Over supper each night, Ryder would tell her the checklist of what he'd accomplished and always end it with a frown that he wished he could have gotten more done. Why was he so hard on himself?

"And the water?" Dad asked.

"I'm sure he's set up the water, too. You do know I don't ride out there with him, right?" she teased. "I take care of the girls."

"Aw, I know." His cheeks grew pink as he chuckled. "I've been thinking about the place a lot lately."

"I get it. You miss it."

His cell phone rang. "It's Mason. I'm going to take this. I'll go outside." He pointed to the hall and answered the phone. "Howdy…"

As his voice faded and the click of the door produced silence, Mom turned to her. "So tell me what's going on with you. Harper and Ivy are so darling, and it sounds like you've been seeing a lot of their daddy."

Her mom had a sparkle in her eye along with a little too much hope. But it was true. She'd been getting to know Ryder better. After supper while they cleaned up, she'd been telling him about her childhood, stories of her and Mia and their games and fights. How they'd bake Christmas cookies for days on end with their mom. How she'd loved growing up in Rendezvous, where everyone knew everyone else. She'd even told him about a few of the elderly shut-ins from church she visited because they'd been so kind to her when she was a girl.

He, in turn, had told her about his college days, working in an upscale office and how he loved California weather but couldn't stand the traffic.

She could no longer pretend she wasn't getting close to Ryder.

"The girls are amazing." She'd skip her mom's statement about seeing a lot of their daddy. "You know the brag books I've been having them make to give to their mother? They're almost done. It's been fun coming up with new projects to put in them. Last week we hiked around the ranch and picked wildflowers. Then we pressed them and glued them to paper. I laminated the papers to add to the books."

"You always were creative like that." Mom held the cup near her lips as happiness lit her eyes.

"Well, I learned from you." A burst of nostalgia made her heart tender. She'd been missing her mom and hadn't realized it. They'd spent so much time together these past years.

Mom leaned forward. "So…when do you get to meet Lily?"

"I don't know. She might be arriving next week. Ryder isn't sure."

"We've watched all her shows."

"Yeah, but remember, I'm just the babysitter. There might not be any reason for me to be there, so I don't know that I'd meet her."

"Well, maybe Ryder could get an autograph…"

"No." Before getting to know him better, Eden would have jumped at the chance of getting Lily Haviland's autograph. But it no longer held any allure for her. The stars in her eyes when it came to the actress had been erased. "Lily is a sore subject with him."

Mom tapped her chin. "Yes, I imagine it would be hard to divorce someone famous."

"It's probably hard to divorce anyone."

"True." She took another sip of her coffee. "But now that I think of it, it has to be difficult when your ex-wife is a beloved actress and on the cover of magazines whenever a new movie comes out."

"Being constantly reminded of your ex when getting groceries or flipping through channels can't be a good feeling."

"Do you think it's one of the reasons he moved to Wyoming?" Mom asked.

"What do you mean?" She hadn't thought about it.

"Well, there are fewer chances of bumping into reminders of Lily out here."

This wasn't helping. She liked to think of Ryder and the girls embarking on a new life here, not escaping from the old one.

What would happen when the old collided with the new?

What if Ryder fell for Lily all over again when she was here? And the woman would have to be blind not to see how wonderful the girls were and want to be with them. What if Lily and Ryder got back together?

Her time with the girls would come to an end.

A swoosh of sadness hollowed her out. It wasn't just the thought of missing the girls. She'd miss Ryder, too.

Stop thinking about him. He's never been yours.

"He likes being closer to Mason. Maybe he just needed a change." Eden was more than ready to move on to a different subject. "And speaking of changes, I've officially decided to finish my degree. I'm switching my major to education so I can teach elementary school."

"That's great news." Mom cheered up. "I've been praying for God to lead you on the right path. What made you finally decide?"

"Everyone's moving on, and it's time for me to, as well."

"I understand."

"No matter what, though, I plan on staying here." Eden's mind hadn't changed on that, at least.

"Are you sure? Maybe a change of scenery would do you good."

"I'm glad you and Dad are traveling and enjoying yourselves, but I can't imagine leaving my friends, and I'd miss Noah too much."

"We miss him, too." Mom nodded. The sound of the door opening and male voices had them craning their necks to see who'd arrived.

"Look who I found outside." Dad appeared in the living room with Ryder next to him.

She locked gazes with him and a tingling sensation shivered down her spine. He held up a black cardigan. "You forgot your sweater, and since I was stopping at the grocery store, I figured I'd drop it off."

"You didn't have to do that." Eden was ridiculously pleased he had, though.

"Hi, Joanna." Ryder crossed over and bent to give her a hug. "You look great. How's touring the country been going?"

"We love it." She patted the spot next to her on the couch. "Sit down. We need to catch up."

"Oh, no, I can't. I need to pick up the girls from Mason's." He looked like he wanted to, though. "But hey, why don't you all stop by the ranch later? Mason and Brittany are bringing Noah over. Mason's been helping me teach the girls how to ride horses. We're grilling burgers, too. I'd love to have you join us."

Eden opened her mouth to decline, but her dad clapped

Ryder on the back and said, "Sounds great. What time should we come over?"

Wait—what was happening? Why were her parents agreeing to hang out at Ryder's all afternoon?

"Mason's coming over at noon." Ryder's gaze slid to Eden again, and her cheeks grew warm.

"We'll bring a side dish." Mom got the faraway look in her eye that happened whenever she heard there was a potluck. Eden figured they'd be putting together a dish of potato salad within the hour.

"You don't have to bring anything." Ryder shook his head.

"We want to." Mom scoffed as if he'd grown a horn. "It's so nice of you to invite us."

"Well, I'd better get back. See you in a few hours." Ryder cast one final glance at Eden, and she watched him until he turned to leave. Her dad escorted him down the hall, peppering him with questions about the ranch the entire way.

"How many potatoes do you have on hand, Eden?"

She tucked her lips under to keep from laughing. Potato salad. Coming right up.

Thank the good Lord for family. Ryder helped Ivy fasten her safety helmet, while Mason checked Harper's. It was a few minutes before noon. The horses were saddled and ready for the girls. What a perfect day. Blue skies. Nice breeze. The sun heated his bare arms, and every now and then he'd check over his shoulder to see if Eden and her parents had arrived. He wouldn't mind picking Bill's brain about the ranch, and he always felt accepted by Joanna.

But what if Bill was like Granddad, though? Impossible to please. Would the man think Ryder wasn't doing a good job?

"It's too tight, Daddy." Ivy looked nervous. "Can I play with Cutie instead?"

"I thought you liked riding Nugget last week." He hoisted her into his arms so their faces were level. She curled her body into his chest.

"I did, but…"

"Hey there, Skeeter." Eden's father marched over to Harper with a big grin. Ryder must have missed their truck pull up. He instantly searched for Eden. Didn't see her. Had she stayed home? He hoped not.

"I'm Harper. Not Skeeter." She wore her most serious face.

Bill tweaked a lock of hair poking out from under her helmet. "Harper, you say? I thought you were Skeeter. Next you'll be telling me that girl in your daddy's arms isn't Catfish."

Harper broke into a loud giggle. "No, silly, that's Ivy."

"Ivy?" Bill scratched his chin. "I don't think so. Looks like Catfish to me."

"Grandpa!" Noah raced to Bill, and Bill caught him up in his arms.

"Spurs!" Bill kissed Noah's cheek. "You're a sight for sore eyes."

Ivy wriggled for Ryder to set her down, and he obliged. She ran to Harper and they looked up at Bill. "That's not Spurs. That's Noah."

Noah hugged Bill's neck, and the man let out a throaty laugh. Joanna came up next to Bill and held out her arms to the twins.

"Look at you two. You've gotten so tall and pretty." Joanna pointed to Ivy. "Let me guess. You're Ivy, right?"

Ivy nodded. Joanna turned to Harper. "And Harper. I'd know you any day."

The girls exchanged pleased glances. Ryder had to give it to Eden's mom—she could tell the girls apart better than most people, and she'd been around them on only a handful of occasions.

"And how is my Noah?" Joanna asked. Bill set Noah down.

"I'm great! Daddy's teaching Harper and Ivy how to ride horses, and I'm helping." He lifted his chin proudly. "They're my cousins."

"I know, isn't it wonderful?"

"Did you bring the camper? Does it still have a special bed for me? Did you buy popsicles?" Noah asked. "I want to go in it."

"My, my." Joanna laughed. "You have a lot of questions. The RV is at the campground. Grandpa drove his truck."

Noah's face fell, then he asked, "Where's Auntie Eden?"

"She's putting the potato salad in the fridge. She'll be right out."

Joanna hugged Ryder. "We're thankful you're taking such good care of the place." She patted his cheek, and the maternal gesture filled a longing he'd pushed away years ago.

Most of the time, he didn't think about the fact he was an orphan. His grandparents had raised him after his parents died in a car accident when he was a week old. But having Joanna here treating him almost like he was part of the family touched him. Mason was his only family, and since Lily was estranged from her parents, the twins had no grandparents in their lives.

For the first time, Ryder grasped how much his girls were missing. And it made him sad.

"Good to see you, son." Bill pulled Mason into a half embrace, clapping him on the back. "Need some help?"

Mason grinned. "Yeah, we're getting these two up to speed riding horses. They're Wyoming girls now."

"We'd better giddyup and get 'em riding, then." Bill winked at Ivy.

"My kitty needs me." Ivy's pitiful eyes made Ryder almost cave and tell her she could skip the lessons today. He didn't want to push her too hard. He knew riding the horse intimidated her.

"A kitty, you say?" Bill stood before her. "I'm scared of cats."

"Scared?" Her expression broke into astonishment. "Of a kitty? Mine is real nice, Grandpa Bill. She's white and fluffy and purrs and loves to sit on your chest when you're trying to sleep. You'd like her."

Bill shook his head. "She sounds nice, Catfish, but kittens have claws. She'll scratch me."

"She's scratched me." Ivy twisted her lips. "But it didn't hurt too bad."

"You're braver than me," Bill said. "Now, see, riding a horse doesn't scare me. I've ridden them since I was knee-high. But petting a kitten?" He had a grim look on his face.

"Grandpa Bill, you don't need to be scared." Ivy took his hand in hers. "I'll hold Cutie and you can pet her."

"You'd do that for me?" He seemed to think it over. "Okay. But I'd feel better if I could spend some time out here with the horses first. They help me feel calm, you know what I mean? Why don't you get on your horse and I'll lead it for a while? It'll help my nerves."

Ivy gave Nugget a skeptical glance. Then she pulled

back her little shoulders. "If I get on the horse, do you promise to pet Cutie?"

Lines deepened in his forehead as he nodded. "I promise."

Bill took Ivy's hand, let her into the corral and explained to her how to mount the horse. Mason was already leading Harper around the corral. Ryder leaned against the fence and watched in awe as Ivy listened to the man and followed his instructions. Bill was a gem.

"They look like naturals."

Ryder almost jumped. He hadn't noticed Eden approach. With a quick scan, he noticed Joanna and Brittany deep in conversation walking toward the patio. Which left him and Eden alone.

"Your dad just pulled off something I never thought I'd see." He nodded to where Bill continued to talk to Ivy up on Nugget as they made their way around. Ivy giggled loudly. "She's not afraid up there."

The back of Eden's hair lifted in the slight breeze, and her profile was serene. "He's great with kids. He taught me how to ride, and trust me, I was a reluctant rider."

"Did you learn here?" He shifted to face her.

"Yes. Right here in this corral, to be exact. I don't remember much. I know Dad had taken me riding with him since I was old enough to walk, but he must have decided it was time for me to ride solo when I was four or five. I was scared and stubborn."

"You?" He laughed. "I can't picture you scared or stubborn."

"Oh, I can be both." She smiled. "What about you? When did you learn to ride?"

"I'm not sure." Vague recollections of his gruff grandfather came to mind, riding in silence over the hills and plains of the sheep farm in Montana where he grew up. "I feel like I've always been riding."

"Like Noah," Eden said, pointing to the boy.

Mason had brought over Noah's horse in a trailer, and the kid was a natural, the expression on his face pure joy.

"What was the name of your first horse?" he asked.

"Dixie." She grinned. "Yours?"

"Coal. Needless to say, he was pure black. A beautiful horse." His granddad might have been a man of few words and high standards, but he'd made sure Ryder had the best horse he could afford.

As the kids rode, he and Eden shared tales of growing up in the country. An hour passed by and the lessons were finished. Ryder reluctantly peeled himself away from Eden to help Mason and Bill unsaddle the horses.

"Noah! Harper! Ivy!" Joanna called. "We're making cupcakes. Why don't you come help us?"

"Yay!" The trio raced to the patio.

"I'm going to help them." Eden hitched her thumb to the house.

He wanted her to stay. Had enjoyed her easy presence next to him. Liked sharing childhood memories. But Mason and Bill approached, and she was already walking away.

"I've missed this place." Bill looked around. His straw cowboy hat tipped to the sky.

"We can ride around, check it out if you'd like." It would give Ryder the chance to ask him more about the ranch.

"Don't have to ask me twice." Bill grinned. He cocked his head toward Mason. "You up for it?"

"On a day like this?" Mason spread his arms wide. "What are we waiting for?"

In no time at all, the three of them were riding horseback out to where the cattle grazed. Bill pointed out land-marks, like the gully where he'd found a calf half-eaten by coyotes years ago and the plain where the pronghorn liked to cross. Ryder enjoyed listening to him and Mason talk about the land.

Soon they were checking cows. Bill grew quiet. Just barked out observations, like "Keep an eye on the seventy-seven tag. Phlegmy eyes."

Ryder approached a calf he'd been keeping tabs on. Was it his imagination or was it losing weight?

"He's got an abscess," Bill said. "We'll need to lance it."

"Where?" Ryder strained to see any lumps, but the calf hid behind his mother. "Is that why he's losing weight?"

"Under here." Bill raised his chin and pointed to the side of his neck. "From my experience, yes. Probably hurts him to nurse. You rope the head. I'll get the heels. When I've got him, you'll have to keep the rope tight so I can lance it. We'll get him some penicillin and he should be good to go."

Ryder followed Bill's instructions. Soon he was grip-ping the rope as Bill lanced the abscess quickly before giving the calf medicine. In no time flat, the calf was back on its feet, trotting over to his mama.

"Wow. I'm impressed. If that was a sporting event, you two would win." Mason pretended to applaud them.

"Pshaw, that's nothing." Bill looked especially pleased with himself. "It's nice to know I still got it, though."

"You've still got it, all right." The three of them contin-ued to check more cows until Mason's cell phone rang. He answered it, and after a few *yes*es and *sure*s, he hung up.

"Time to head back. The kids want Grandpa to have cupcakes with them."

Bill let out a guffaw. "The only thing better than riding

out across this land is having cupcakes with those kid-
dos. I made Ivy a promise to pet her kitten, too. Let's go."

As they rode back to the stables, Ryder's heart was
full. The Lord's blessings were overflowing. He'd enjoy
them while they lasted.

What a terrific afternoon. Eden wiped the crumbs off
Ryder's countertop while her parents talked to Mason
and Brittany in the hall. Ryder was in the sunroom with
the kids and the kittens, and she pretended—just for
a moment—this was her house again. As soon as the
thought occurred, she pictured Ryder coming into the
kitchen and wrapping his arms around her from behind.
Resting his chin on her shoulder, and her laughing, turning her face just so…

"Change of plans." Mom breezed into the kitchen.
"Your dad and I are taking the kids to Mason and Brittany's for a while. We'll be back around six to help cook
the burgers. Love you!" And she trotted away before
Eden could respond.

Tossing the washcloth into the sink, Eden pursued her
to the front porch while the others headed to their vehi-
cles. "Wait, I'll come with you."

Mom smiled. "You stay here with Ryder. Take a
break."

"I don't need a break."

"Yes, you do." Mom walked ahead with a backward
wave.

"What just happened?" Ryder came up and stood next
to Eden as doors slammed shut and engines roared to life.

"I have no idea."

"One minute everyone's having a good time, stuffing
their faces full of cupcakes…" He frowned. "It's like they
wanted to get away from us."

"Do I smell?" She turned her head and sniffed. "I'm wearing body spray."

"You smell great." He stepped closer to her. "And I don't think it was something I said."

"No, they weren't offended. They're…happy."

He blew out a breath. "Well, I guess it's their loss."

"Yeah." Now what was she supposed to do? Her parents were gone. Her nephew had left. The twins weren't around, either. There was no reason to stay. "I guess I should get out of your hair."

"No way. And leave me all alone? Then I'll really feel like a leper."

"What are we going to do?" She wrung her hands.

He considered for a moment before snapping his fingers "What do you say we get out of here for a while?"

"Where will we go?"

"Anywhere. I'm new to the area. Show me something I haven't seen before."

She thought about it. "You've been to all the stores in town. And the park. Nothing new there."

"True."

A vision of her special place outside town crowded her mind. No, she couldn't take him there. It was special for a reason. Private. But the longer the silence stretched, the more she realized she wanted him to see it.

"I know where we'll go." Nervousness tightened her chest, but she tried to tamp it down. "Do you want to drive?"

"Sure. Do we need anything?"

"A blanket and some snacks wouldn't hurt."

"Coming right up." He wiggled his eyebrows, and she shook her head, trying not to laugh.

What would he think of it? It was just a flat top of a

hill with a spectacular view. Maybe Ryder wouldn't appreciate it.

She hoped he would.

She washed her hands and did a once-over of the kitchen to make sure everything had been put away.

"All set." Ryder held a small cooler in one hand, and a plaid blanket was tucked under his arm. He spun his keys on his index finger. "Where are we going, Captain?"

"Captain?" She gestured for them to go outside. "I'm not taking you on a boat ride."

"And here I was hoping…"

As Ryder helped her into the passenger side of his truck, she tried not to notice his strong hand at her elbow. He jogged around to the driver's side. Soon they were driving along back roads. Neither spoke much. They didn't need to. It was a beautiful, peaceful day. If she could bottle it, she would.

She gave him directions, and miles later, they'd parked on a grass lane and began hiking.

"What are those white flowers?" Ryder asked as they climbed the hill.

"Cushion phlox. Pretty, aren't they?" She breathed in the fresh air and took in the wildflowers dotting the prairie grass. "You'll see clusters of them all summer long. The taller bluish-purple flowers are lupine."

"I know lupine. If our sheep ate too much of them, they got sick."

"Really? Tell me about raising sheep." Eden kept a moderate pace. They'd almost reached the top of the hill. "How in the world did you go from sheep ranching in Montana to financial planner in LA?"

His eyes crinkled as he smiled. "It's different from raising cattle, that's for sure."

"Raising sheep or living in LA?"

"Both." The land leveled off, and Ryder stopped in his tracks. He looked over the valley and the acres before them. Mountains in the distance broke up the blue sky. "Wow. What is this?"

"My special place." The words were out before she could analyze if it was wise to reveal that part of herself. "If it wasn't owned by the federal government, I would buy it. I love this land. Don't worry, we're not trespassing. The Bureau of Land Management allows public access."

"It is special." He pointed to the left. "Look, pronghorn. They're running."

The sight of them leaping and bounding over the ground always sent a thrill through Eden, and today was no exception. "Breathtaking."

"It is." His voice grew husky, and she glanced at him. He was looking at her with a serious expression, and it sent heat to her cheeks.

"Here, I'll spread out the blanket." She reached for it as he handed it to her. Their fingers touched, spiraling her nerves to high alert. Maybe she should have opted for camping chairs instead. She shook out the blanket and let it float over the grass. Ryder stretched the corners, and they both sat down.

"Why is this your special spot?" he asked, leaning back on his elbows with his legs stretched out before him. He wore jeans, a T-shirt, cowboy boots and a straw hat.

He was all lean muscles.

"You first. I asked about raising sheep." She wasn't sure she could put into words what this spot meant to her.

"By the time my parents died and my grandparents took me in as a baby, Granddad's sheep ranch was already declining. I helped him out at a young age. I remember him taking me out to the sheep wagons in the summer to check on the herders and bring them supplies. I can still see those trailers in the middle of nowhere. Loneliest things I could imagine."

Eden could picture it. "Did you ever stay in one?"

"Me? No." He shook his head. "I stayed on the main ranch. In the winter, I'd help out in the lambing shed. I learned a lot about life there. My favorite job was hand-feeding the orphans."

An image appeared in her mind of Ryder as a boy holding a lamb on his lap and feeding it a bottle.

"How did you end up in California?" She wanted to learn more about him. Get a complete picture of the man next to her.

"After Grandma died, there was no reason for me to stay in Montana. I got a scholarship to Cal State, interned for a financial-planning firm catering to Hollywood stars, and they hired me right out of school."

The last part sounded like a fairy tale—glamorous, adventurous. Eden couldn't imagine taking off to California at such a young age.

"Was it hard for you?" she asked. "Losing your grandparents, setting out on your own. I mean, California is a long way from Montana."

He considered it for a few moments. "Yes, but I didn't know any better. And I knew God would guide me. One thing I'm thankful for? My grandparents took me to church. I don't know that I'd have my faith if it wasn't for them."

"My parents laid the foundation for my faith, too," Eden said. "After Mia died, we grew closer, got through it together. When life gets me down, Mom tells me to pray. When life looks up, Mom tells me to pray. She gets on my nerves sometimes, if I'm being honest." She chuckled.

"Your mom's a wise woman." He shifted to his side, facing her. "So, your turn… This spot?"

This spot. The place she always ran to when life was too much.

"I come here when I can't take it anymore." She didn't look at him.

"Take what?" he asked quietly.

"Life." She turned to him then. "I was away at college when I found out Mia was diagnosed with cancer. I came home for Christmas break, and I remember trudging up this hill in a foot of snow and sinking to my knees and begging God to save her. A couple of months after she died, Gabby and I decided to celebrate Mia's life by camping up here. It was summer, and the black sky, the millions of stars overhead and the peace of this place helped heal my heart. I come here whenever life gets to be too much."

"I can see why."

"I came here when I found out my parents wanted to sell the ranch."

"Ah…" His expression was sympathetic as he pushed up to a seated position. "You probably came here when you found out I was buying it, too."

"I did."

"You didn't like me."

"I didn't know you."

"Do you know me now?"

"Yes. I think so, at least." She licked her lips, nervous all of a sudden. Undercurrents swam beneath their conversation.

"Did you leave anyone special behind at college?" His caramel eyes captured her, and she inhaled sharply.

Someone special? Yeah, right. She'd never had a real boyfriend. It wasn't that she'd lacked for dates in high school to school dances and such. And a few guys had asked her out in college. She'd even said yes to them.

But no one had captured her interest. Not the way she'd hoped.

"No."

"Why aren't you seeing anyone?" He sounded curious, not judgmental. "I don't get it."

It was on the tip of her tongue to snap that it certainly wasn't by choice, but maybe that wasn't true. She'd been blaming the men in town for not being interested in her. The truth was she wasn't interested in them, either.

With a slight shrug, she gazed out over the prairie. "They aren't into me, and I'm not into them."

He shifted slightly closer. "High standards?"

"Them?" Her head told her to lean away and create some distance between them. But her body remained frozen in place. "Or me?"

"You." His glance fell to her mouth, and she shivered.

"No, not high standards. More like unrealistic expectations."

His mouth curved into a smile, and her pulse pounded like the pronghorn herd over the prairie they'd watched earlier.

"You're not the only one, Eden." The sound of her name on his lips flashed goose bumps over her skin. "I'm the king of unrealistic expectations."

"I'm sorry, Ryder. I guess real life caught up with both of us."

His eyes darkened and his cheek muscle flexed. "I wonder…"

What? What did he wonder? She got the impression he wanted to kiss her. She shouldn't be having these feelings, but she wanted him to kiss her. Desperately.

He squinted as if he'd had a thought he didn't want. Then he shook his head and eased back. "No."

Disappointment hit her hard.

It was better this way. She was under no illusions. She wasn't his type.

Even so, it sure felt like another unrealistic expectation had just popped.

Chapter Nine

These feelings for Eden were another unrealistic expectation waiting to destroy him.

Tuesday morning Ryder and Chris rode behind several cows and their young calves, encouraging them to join the rest of the herd. It was a cool, windy day, and he wore a black sweatshirt to protect himself from the chill. He wished he had something he could put on to protect his heart from these inconvenient feelings he had for Eden.

"Looks like we missed a few." Chris nodded to another small bunch of cows and their calves hiding behind a hill near a stretch of cottonwoods.

Ryder followed him to the group, and together they pushed them along with the rest of the stragglers. As his horse trotted, he kept an eye on the cattle and let his mind wander.

He'd enjoyed having Eden's parents over on Saturday. They'd treated Harper and Ivy like they were family. They'd treated him like he was, too. And ever since, he'd been thinking he liked the idea of being part of a bigger family. He liked the thought of the girls having grandparents.

But that desire took a distant second to what he'd felt

when Eden had taken him to that beautiful piece of land. He could see why she was drawn to the place, and he'd been honored when she'd opened up her private thoughts to him. Her claim about having unrealistic expectations had struck him to the core.

He'd been let down by unrealistic expectations his entire life.

And for whatever reason, acknowledging it there—on the hill overlooking the prairie full of grass and wildflowers—had sent his attraction to Eden to a whole new level.

He'd almost kissed her.

The only thing that had stopped him was remembering the twins' third birthday when Lily had told him she was leaving him. He'd been blindsided. Looking back, he wasn't sure why. They'd had problems for years. The relationship had been all but over a few months after the twins were born.

But still…hearing Lily tell him she was leaving him, watching the movers come and pack her things, knowing she would be living with another man from that moment forward… It had taken an emotional toll.

He couldn't afford another crippling emotional event at this point in his life. The twins needed him to be strong. They needed their daddy. They certainly didn't have a mother to rely on.

"If we push 'em to the gate, we can do a quick check on the forty-five tag." Chris looked bright-eyed today. "Is something wrong?"

"No, I'm fine." He had to get his mind back on the cattle where it belonged. "I'll open the gate."

When they'd gotten the cattle through, they checked on the calf and headed back.

"Is it okay for me to kick off a little early on Friday?" Chris asked.

"Sure. You have plans with Trevor, right?" Ryder asked as they loped across the land. Yesterday, Chris had asked for the weekend off. Ryder had no problem giving it to him. He could handle this place without Chris for a few days. He still had part-time ranch hands to help out, and if he got desperate, he could always call Mason.

"Yep. We're driving to Dubois for the rodeo. He's been texting me his picks for bareback bronc riding." Chris laughed, and Ryder was struck at how much younger he appeared. Chris often seemed to have the world on his shoulders. "That kid. He's already competing in break-away roping, bareback steer riding and even bull riding. He hopes to join the high school team when he's older."

"My nephew's been mutton busting." Ryder couldn't imagine the twins competing in a rodeo at their age, although Harper would probably be a natural fit. "Did you teach him how to ride?"

"Of course. I had him mutton busting and barrel racing by the time he was in first grade. Kid loves the rodeo."

"Is your ex giving you any more trouble?"

"When doesn't she?" He wiped his forehead and shook his head. "I'm sure I'll get a text Friday morning about a distant cousin's birthday party or whatnot. I'm not bending this time."

The barns came into view. Lily was supposed to be arriving on Friday. Mandy had emailed him the flight time and the address of the luxury log cabin Lily would be staying in. He still didn't think she'd actually show up.

Maybe he, like Chris, was bending too much when it came to her. Everything was on Lily's terms. What was the alternative, though? He didn't know, and he didn't want to find out.

* * *

"There. You're all set." Eden tied an apron with images of kittens chasing balls of yarn around Ivy's waist Tuesday afternoon. She'd already tied Harper's pony-themed apron. Eden and her mom had sewed the aprons on Sunday after church. Mom had come up with the idea and, frankly, done most of the work. Spending the day with her mother had lifted Eden's spirits, not to mention it had helped take her mind off the near kiss with Ryder.

She was falling too hard, too fast. It was better to put the brakes on now, rather than be demolished later. At least she'd had the gumption to not eat supper with him and the girls last night. She didn't plan on eating with them anymore moving forward.

"What are we making today?" Harper asked. The girls waited in eager anticipation in Nicole Taylor's small kitchen. Eden had babysat Phoebe all morning, and Gabby had picked her up right after lunch. It was just Eden and the twins baking this afternoon.

Nicole was a pretty blonde with green eyes and a kind way about her. She wore a cute pink apron that said Bakers Gotta Bake on it.

"I heard you two like chocolate." Nicole watched them carefully. They yelled "Yes!" and clapped. She grinned. "We're making a triple-layer chocolate cake."

Ivy turned and took Harper's hands in hers. They jumped in excitement.

"Are the babies gonna help?" Harper grew serious.

"No, they're still too little."

"Can I hold one after we make the cake?" Ivy asked.

"I don't see why not." Nicole's smile lit her eyes. "They seem to like you."

The triplets were all bouncing in ExerSaucers in the

dining area. Eden took a seat near them while Nicole instructed the girls.

"Okay, Ivy, why don't you pour the sugar into the mixer. And Harper, unwrap this stick of butter..."

Henry, the baby with the darkest hair, thumped the meat of his palms on the tray and yelled when a rubber squeeze toy shaped like a penguin went flying. Eden picked it up and gave it back to him. His gummy grin dripped with drool. He was the cutest thing she'd seen all day. And that was saying something considering she was surrounded by cute.

Eli was parked next to Henry, and his little tongue stuck out as he concentrated on trying to move a squeaky tiger down a curved, plastic-coated wire. Amelia was bouncing and chirping and smiling away.

Eden really wanted a baby. As much as she tried to push the urge away, it was still there. It had been there for years.

Don't go there. Think about something else—think about something you can actually have. Like a teaching career.

While a part of her was excited at the thought of getting her degree, another part ached at what felt like goodbye. Making the final decision to go back to school felt like she was locking the door to her other dreams—the ones of becoming a wife and mother. Her logic might not make sense, but she couldn't shake the feeling, just the same.

"Our mommy's coming on Friday," Ivy said to Nicole.

"She is? That's wonderful!" Nicole's enthusiasm must have pleased Ivy because she beamed.

"She's not staying at our house, though." Harper was more matter-of-fact.

"That's okay." Nicole handed Harper a whisk and gestured for her to whisk the dry ingredients they'd added to a separate bowl. "The important thing is you get to spend time with her."

"I want to show her how I can ride a horse." Harper whisked a little too hard and some flour went flying. "Sorry! I didn't mean it."

"It's fine, Harper." Nicole chuckled. "I do it all the time. Baking is messy."

Eden's heart swelled in appreciation for her friend. The woman was one of a kind. She'd lost her husband when she was only a few months pregnant, then she'd moved back to Rendezvous and had the triplets. Last Christmas, she'd fallen in love with Judd Wilson, the cowboy who owned the ranch her cabin sat on. Nicole and Judd were engaged but hadn't set the date yet. And even with her hands so full, Nicole had still carved out time to make two little girls very happy today.

Amelia started cooing, "Ooh, ooh, ooh," and Eden laughed.

"After the cake is all done, we're going to put it in a pretty pink box to take home." Nicole turned the mixer on low.

"You mean we get to keep it?" Harper asked.

"Yes."

"Daddy likes chocolate." Ivy nodded.

Harper peered into the mixer. "Can we lick the bowl?"

"We'd better not." As Nicole gave them tips about not eating batter with raw eggs, Eden's mind drifted back to Saturday.

Taking Ryder to her special place had been a mistake. Spending the afternoon alone with him had deepened her connection to him, and her feelings had already been inching too close to begin with. Later that night, after the cookout, when she was alone in her apartment, it had hit her that Ryder didn't have family. Not the way she did.

He had no parents. His grandparents were gone. Besides Mason, Ryder didn't have extended family to depend on when life got rough.

Eden had always been close to her mother and father. She still was.

Maybe she'd overreacted when her parents sold the ranch. After all, a house was just a bunch of walls if her loved ones weren't there with her.

For the next few minutes the mixer whirred loudly, then Nicole turned it off and instructed the girls how to pour the batter into three round pans. Soon, the cakes were in the oven and the timer was set.

"Can I hold a baby now?" Ivy steepled her hands with the tips of her fingers below her chin.

"After we wash our hands. Eden, would you mind taking Eli out and setting him in the living room? There's a quilt on the floor." Nicole guided the girls down the hall to wash their hands in the bathroom. "I'll be right there."

Eden lifted Eli out and cuddled him to her chest. He stared at her with a serious expression, and she kissed his forehead. "You are way too cute, little guy."

She brought him over to the quilt and talked to him for a while before setting him down, and before she knew it, Nicole had carried over Amelia and Henry.

"Sit on the couch, Ivy, and I'll hand her to you." Once Ivy was settled, Nicole placed Amelia in her open arms.

"She's heavy." Ivy smiled down at the child and kissed the top of her head. "She's prettier than my baby. I wish I could take her home."

Nicole laughed. "That's nice of you to say. Maybe when you're older, you'll babysit her. You never know."

"I'd like that." Ivy hugged the child. "Would you like me to babysit you, Amelia?"

"Harper, would you like to hold Henry?"

"No thanks." Harper got down on the quilt and spread out on her tummy. She propped her elbows on the floor and rested her chin on her palms, with her feet in the air. "Can this one crawl?"

"He can."

"Why isn't he?" Harper asked.

"He's playing."

"Are you gonna let him eat that puppy?" She seemed concerned he was chewing on the ear of the stuffed animal.

"Yes."

"Can I set her on the quilt?" Ivy asked. "I want to play down there, too."

Nicole took Amelia from her and set her on the quilt with the boys. The twins played with the triplets while Eden and Nicole watched them and chitchatted.

"I've decided to take online classes this fall." Eden figured it was time to start getting her friends used to the idea. She'd already told Gabby last night.

"You are?" Nicole curled her knees to the side where she sat opposite Eden on the couch. "What kind of classes?"

"I'm going to finish my degree." Saying the words out loud bolstered her courage. "I'm switching majors. I want to be a teacher."

"You'll be fantastic! Remind me what your original major was."

"Early education. Preschool, mainly."

"Ah." Nicole's smile encouraged her. "What changed your mind?"

"It's time." And those two words spread peace to the

nooks and crannies clinging to her old dreams. "Mason's moved on. Gabby's moved on. You've moved on. It's time for me to move on, too."

"Have you moved on where it counts?" Nicole pointed to her chest. "In here?"

"Yes." It was true. She'd moved on from Mia's death.

"That's all that matters. Tell me everything."

Eden kept an eye on the girls, who were happily giving the triplets toys, as she filled Nicole in on what steps she needed to take to get her degree.

"I'm really impressed," Nicole said. "But I hope you aren't planning on moving away."

"Oh, no. This is my home."

"Good." Nicole cast a sly glance at the twins, then raised innocent eyebrows. "Rendezvous has a lot to offer."

Heat rushed to Eden's cheeks. "All I'm asking for is a full-time job. Preferably teaching younger grades."

"Nothing else?" Nicole gave a quick jerk of her head toward the girls.

"No." But it was a lie. Eden wanted it all, including Ryder and the girls.

One of the triplets let out a cry, and Nicole excused herself.

An uncomfortable thought weighed on her chest. If Ryder didn't have the twins, would she still be drawn to him?

She tried to picture him without the girls and couldn't. They were a package deal.

Why was she thinking about it anyhow?

Ryder *did* have the girls.

And he had a beautiful, glamorous ex-wife along with a firm resolution he was never getting married again.

So regardless if she was falling for him and wanted

to be part of the girls' lives, it wasn't going to happen. She had no say in it.

The inevitability of it all crashed down on her. Their time together would end in a few short months. She would not be a permanent part of their lives.

Always the babysitter. Never the bride.

Ryder stood in front of Eden's door at eight o'clock that night. The girls were watching an animated film with Noah at Mason's house. All day he'd been looking forward to having supper with Eden and then talking to her in private. But Eden had left as soon as he'd finished his ranch chores. He really needed to speak to her alone. There was still a good chance Lily would cancel her visit, but if she didn't, Ryder needed backup with the girls on Saturday and Sunday morning.

He knocked twice.

She opened the door, and her eyes grew round. "What are you doing here?"

Not the most welcoming words, but he'd take them. "Can we talk?"

Her eyelashes fluttered, but she moved aside to let him in. She'd changed into leggings and a long exercise shirt. Her slim gracefulness captivated him as he followed her to the living room.

"Is something going on? Is it the girls?" Eden sat down, concern radiating from her brown eyes.

"No, nothing's wrong." He took a seat on the couch. "It's about Lily's visit."

"Oh, right. I actually meant to speak to you about it earlier, and it slipped my mind. Don't worry—I know it's important for the girls to spend some good quality time with their mom. I'll stay away."

"I would never ask you to stay away. In fact, I'm asking the opposite. I was hoping you could help me out this weekend."

"Help you? How?"

"Chris has the weekend off, and one of my ranch hands might not be able to help me out, which means I need to do the things he normally does on Saturday and Sunday morning. So regardless if Lily comes—"

"If she comes? Did she say she might not?"

"No." He kept his voice even. "But a last-minute cancellation is always possible. And either way, she might not get to the ranch early enough for me to leave the girls to check on the cattle."

Understanding washed away the worries on Eden's face. "Oh, I understand now. Yes, I can come early both days. I'll stay with them while you deal with the ranch. Then, when Lily arrives, I'll get out of everyone's hair."

Get out of their hair? What was she talking about? He immediately glanced at her silky hair and wanted to run his fingers through it.

"You're not in anyone's hair. You wouldn't be in the way. You're an important part of our lives."

She looked stricken. What had he said now? It had been a good long while since he'd put his foot in his mouth with her. He didn't even know how he'd offended her this time, but it was obvious by her pale face that he had.

"Look, Eden," he said, moving his neck back and forth to work out the kinks. "Lily might seem like this special movie star, but she's just a person the same as you and me. When I met her, I was starstruck, so I get it. And the fact she even gave me the time of day blew my mind back then. Lily has a way about her—she has charisma. She can be nice, generous. She pulls you into her orbit." He still remembered that light, anything-is-possible feeling he'd gotten when they'd first met.

"She's always been one of my favorite actresses." Eden averted her eyes.

"Most people put Lily on a pedestal. Maybe we all expect her to be as amazing as the characters she plays on television and in movies. I don't know."

A sense of heaviness weighed on his shoulders. He'd been over every nuance in their relationship a hundred times or more. At first he'd blamed himself. Then he'd blamed her.

But the truth was they both were to blame.

"Have you ever been in love?" he asked quietly.

Eden froze. Blinked. Didn't answer.

Of course she'd been in love. That was why she wasn't married—she'd loved and lost, too. Jealousy built inside him, spinning like a tornado at the thought of anyone letting her down.

She stood and crossed to the window, looking out onto the neighboring yard with her arms over her chest. Ryder padded over to stand behind her. He set his hands on her shoulders. Her head jerked to look back at him, but she didn't step away from his touch.

"Whoever he is—was—he doesn't deserve you." His voice was low, husky.

Lily had been smoke and mirrors.

Eden was genuine. The real deal.

She turned then. Slowly. Deliberately. But she didn't create distance between them. They were only inches from each other, and she looked up at him through those piercing, soulful eyes.

His heart slammed into his ribs. He caressed her upper arms as he drew her closer. He couldn't look away from her lips.

Her hands crept up and slipped around his neck. Uncertainty and fascination warred in her eyes. He couldn't take the suspense a minute longer. Dropping his hands to her waist, he lowered his mouth to hers.

She was delicate but strong, soft but firm. Impressions raced through his mind—of his lonely childhood, the sheep trailers in the middle of nowhere, the hollowness he'd felt after Grandma died, the kick in the gut when Lily left him—and all of them spun together and burst into tiny pieces as the kiss promised he never needed to be alone again.

Eden was who he'd been waiting for his entire life.

And he hadn't known it until now.

He kissed her deeply, reveling in the curve of her body near his. Finally, he broke away from the kiss. The revelations he'd just learned still thrummed in his head.

He'd promised himself he wasn't falling in love again. No marriage for him. He wasn't putting himself through the pain of trusting someone and getting cheated on and discarded ever again.

But Eden made him want to.

Even if he lost it all.

Chapter Ten

"Dandy jumped on my flowerpot!" Tears swam in Ivy's eyes.

Eden scooped up the rambunctious kitten and set it on the floor of the family room, where she'd arranged a long folding table. A lime-green felt mouse caught her eye, and she tossed it across the room, where the kitten sprinted after it. The girls were painting flowerpots for their mother, and tomorrow they'd fill them with potting soil and plant gerbera daisies to give to Lily. Well, they would be if Eden could concentrate.

Her head was filled with memories of last night's kiss.

"There. Dandy's gone." Eden scrunched her nose to smile at Ivy.

When Ryder had assumed she'd been in love and claimed the man didn't deserve her, she'd almost laughed—she'd never been in love. But this morning, after a sleepless night, she'd realized she was wrong.

She was in love.

And the revelation colored everything, because nothing could come of it. Especially after hearing him talk about Lily's good traits. Sure, he'd accepted their marriage was over. But what woman could ever live up to his ex-wife? Not her.

"Everything's dirty!" Ivy had been emotionally fragile yesterday, and today everything was setting her off. Eden could only assume Lily's impending visit was the cause.

"Dandy didn't mean it, Ivy." Harper slid out of the chair and hugged her sister.

"I know." Ivy sniffed, wiping under her eyes. "But I want the flowers to be perfect for Mommy."

"They don't have to be perfect, Ivy." Eden walked around the table and kneeled between the twins. She put her arms around each of their shoulders. "Your mom is going to love them because you gave them to her."

"It's ugly now." Ivy's voice broke as she pointed to the colorfully painted clay pot with drips of paint smeared down the side.

Eden reached for a roll of paper towels, tore one off and carefully wiped the smears. "There. All better."

Ivy inspected it and let out a shaky breath.

"You know you don't have to be perfect for your mommy to love you, right?" Eden asked.

Ivy averted her eyes, but Harper glued her attention to Eden.

"What's the book the pastor reads from every Sunday in church?" Eden asked as she went back to her seat across the table from them.

"The Bible." Harper propped her elbows on the table. Ivy climbed into her chair and slumped.

"Right. And the Bible is God's word. He tells us we can't be perfect, because we all sin. But—" Eden held up her index finger "—since Jesus died for us, we don't have to be perfect. He was perfect for us. He takes away all our sins."

"But that's Jesus." Ivy met her eyes then. "Not Mommy."

"That's true, but I happen to know you have a daddy and mommy who love you very much, and they don't expect you to be perfect, either." As she said it, doubts tiptoed through her mind. Ivy was extremely hard on herself. Had Lily made her feel that way? Or was it a natural reaction to missing her mother?

God, please give me the right words for these children.

"I wish Mommy lived here," Ivy said almost under her breath.

"She's not going to live here, Ivy, even if your pot's perfect." Harper's voice rose sternly.

Ah... A wave of understanding came over Eden. Ivy blamed herself for Lily being gone.

"Girls, let's take a break from painting. Go wash your hands, and when you come back, we're going to sit together and talk."

Neither looked happy about it, but they slunk away to the bathroom anyway. Eden wasn't great at pep talks, but the twins clearly needed one. She could hear them talking from the other room.

"If she likes it here, she'll stay..." Ivy's voice rose.

"She won't."

"She might."

"Mommy never stays."

"This time she will. She'll see Daddy. He's the most handsomest daddy there is, and she'll hug him and he'll say he's sorry, and she'll stay forever."

"She's not gonna." Harper's voice was sharp.

Oh, no. Ivy wanted her parents to get back together. Of course.

The girls wanted their mother here for good. And from everything Ryder had told her, it wasn't going to happen.

An icky sensation climbed her throat. How could she be in love with Ryder when the twins needed Lily?

Oh, Lord, I've been wrong. I haven't been thinking about these precious girls. I've been thinking about myself. I don't know how to reassure them, but they're hurting so badly. Please give me the words to help them. Let me put their needs first.

She took a deep breath and straightened her shoulders. They were in the bathroom scowling at each other, and she herded them back into the family room. The three of them sat on a big comfy chair. Harper laid her head against Eden's upper arm, but Ivy held herself stiffly.

"Girls, I know you're hurting. This isn't easy. Living without your mother isn't easy."

Ivy gazed up at her through watery eyes.

"But I don't want you to doubt her love for you. And I don't want you to doubt your daddy's love, either. They both love you. And you'll always be a family, even if it doesn't look the way you'd hoped."

Ivy seemed skeptical, and Harper burrowed against her arm.

"I wish families always stayed together." Eden was extra thankful for her parents at this moment. "But sometimes they don't, and there's nothing you can do about it."

"But…" Ivy's mouth twisted. "I want Mommy to live here."

"I know, sweetheart." Eden smoothed her hair.

"She's so pretty. Prettier than Cinderella." Ivy looked perplexed. "When Daddy sees her, he'll kiss her and they'll live here together happily ever after." She peered over to Harper. "Won't they, Harper?"

"That's a cartoon." Harper shook her head. "Mommy isn't going to stay here no matter how pretty she is."

"But Daddy can tell her…"

This wasn't going well. And thinking about Ryder seeing his beautiful ex and falling in love with her all over again wasn't helping Eden, either. Because it very well could happen.

"Ivy, you know Mommy has a boyfriend." Harper glared at her sister.

"He's old and ugly!" The girl was on the verge of losing it.

Frankly, Eden was on the verge, too, if this conversation continued much longer.

"It doesn't matter what anyone looks like," Eden said. "What counts is in here." She pointed to her heart. "God looks at the heart, not at your outward appearance. What kind of person you are is what makes you attractive."

"What do you mean?" Harper twirled a section of Eden's hair around her finger.

"Well, what do you love and admire about Ivy?" Eden asked.

"She gives me her best stickers when I'm sad. She lets me sleep with Fluffybear if I have a bad dream."

Eden kissed the top of her head. "And Ivy, what do you love and admire about Harper?"

"She's brave. She doesn't squish the bugs she finds—she makes houses for them—and she jumps off the picnic table even though it's really high. And she always knows when I'm sad. She hugs me."

Okay, it was her turn to get teary eyed. She willed her emotions back in place. "The things you described have nothing to do with your pretty blue eyes or your cute noses, do they?" Eden looked at Ivy, then Harper.

"No." Harper shook her head.

"That's what I mean. Your beauty comes from who you are, not what you look like. And both of you are very beautiful on the inside."

Harper hugged her neck and whispered softly in her ear, "I love you, Auntie Eden."

Sweeter words had never been spoken. She kissed Harper's cheek. "I love you, too." Then she kissed Ivy's cheek. "And I love you."

They hugged her tightly.

"Okay, we'd better get these pots painted. We still have a lot of surprises to prepare for your mommy."

As Eden watched the girls skip over to the table with renewed enthusiasm, her mood plummeted. They hadn't recovered from the divorce, didn't understand why Lily wasn't around, and wanted their parents back together. They needed a delicate touch right now.

It would be cruel to pursue a relationship with Ryder if it meant hurting the twins. She'd keep her feelings hidden, and maybe someday, her love would fade.

"The coast is clear. What's going on?" Ryder checked one more time to verify the girls were far enough away in the backyard so that he and Eden could talk openly. The four of them had eaten turkey sandwiches and pasta salad outside before the girls ran off to chase butterflies. He was glad Eden had stayed for supper. It had been a while since she'd stayed to eat with them. He watched her expectantly. She'd claimed they needed to talk.

He could guess why.

The kiss. The over-the-top, incredible kiss that had left him shaken and confused and more scared of his feelings than ever.

He loved her.

And he couldn't do a thing about it.

What was she going to say? That it was inappropriate for him to have kissed her? He never should have crossed that boundary? She didn't like him that way?

He could handle the first options, but the last one would hurt. It hadn't been that long ago since she told him she wasn't attracted to him because he looked exactly like Mason.

His neck tensed as he waited for her to reject him. Again.

"The girls were wound up today." Her words were so quiet he almost asked her to repeat them. He hadn't been expecting a conversation about the twins.

"I think they—Ivy in particular—are hoping you and Lily will get back together."

Him and Lily? Back together?

The thought was ludicrous and he would have laughed, but Eden's serious expression killed his humor.

"Why would they think that? I don't talk about her. She barely calls or visits." He rubbed his chin. Had Lily said something to make them believe they'd get back together? When could the subject have even come up? He'd been there for every short call, and he hadn't caught a hint of it.

"I think it's a normal reaction of kids whose parents have divorced. Plus, I could be wrong, but it seems as if Ivy is putting a lot of pressure on herself right now."

"What kind of pressure?" His gaze traveled to where the girls crouched over something in the grass. Then they were up and running once more.

"It's almost as if she thinks she has to be perfect—that everything has to be perfect—when Lily comes. I wonder if she blames herself in some way for her mother not being around."

"Why would she think that?" His spine grew rigid. "The problems were between Lily and me. Not the girls."

"It doesn't have to make sense to be true," Eden said softly.

He couldn't argue with that. "I'll talk to them."

"What will you say?" Her eyes held no judgment.

"I don't know. I'll figure something out." He rubbed the back of his neck. How was he supposed to handle this? He didn't know where to start.

Eden seemed withdrawn. Subdued. He knew he was to blame.

"Look, about last night…"

Her wan smile hit him in the chest. "Let's not talk about it. We both know nothing can come of it."

Logic told him she was correct. In fact, he'd told her as much more than once. Told himself the same, too. But hearing it on her lips only made him want to dig in and prove her wrong.

"I care about you." He reached over and covered her hand with his.

"I know." She slipped her hand free. "I also know you have good reasons why you're against a serious relationship. You haven't been shy about them, and I appreciate that you opened up about your marriage. But I think you're right. The twins have different emotional needs at this time."

He should be relieved, but he wasn't. Was this about marriage? The twins? Or her own lack of feelings for him?

"Do me a favor and be extra patient with Ivy." Eden stared at him then. He felt like he was swirling into the depths of her inner world.

She had a heart bigger than the sun.

"I guarantee they're picking flowers for their mother." A smile teased her lips. "You have the most precious, thoughtful daughters."

The truth hit him harder than the stray bull that plowed through the fence last week—Eden would always put the girls' needs above her own, and the fact it was a sacrifice wouldn't even occur to her because she wanted them to be happy.

His throat tightened. He'd never known anyone like Eden. Her love for the twins humbled him, and dejection settled between his shoulders. Eden was a temporary blessing.

He wished things were different. Wished he and the girls could have her forever.

"Do you mind if my mom comes over tomorrow?" Eden asked.

He pulled himself together quickly. "That's fine."

"She enjoys Harper and Ivy. I think she needs a break from all the one-on-one with my dad."

"If she's coming, tell Bill he's welcome to ride out with me if he'd like." Checking the cattle and tooling around the ranch with Eden's dad would take his mind off his problems.

"Daddy, Daddy!" Harper's cheeks were pink and her eyes sparkled as she ran to him with her palms cupped together. Ivy followed behind with a bouquet of wildflowers clenched in her hand.

"What?" He forced himself to grin.

"I found a caterpillar!"

Ivy poked Harper's hands. "Show him."

She cautiously opened her hands, and a fuzzy pale yellow caterpillar inched up her fingers. She giggled. "It tickles."

Ivy tentatively petted it. "It's soft. Not as soft as Cutie, though."

"Can I keep it?" Her eyes shined and her toothy smile pleaded.

"I don't think so." Ryder tried to let her down gently. "Kittens eat caterpillars."

Her face fell, but she nodded. "I don't want him to get eaten."

"You can play with him for a while outside, though, okay?"

"Okay." She wrangled it back onto her palm and cupped her other hand over it again. "Come on, Ivy! Let's make a house out of sticks for him."

Ivy thrust the flowers to Eden. "These are for you, Auntie Eden."

Ryder noted the slight dampness in Eden's eyes and her generous hug for Ivy.

"Thank you," Eden said. "They're beautiful. You're so thoughtful."

Ivy beamed. Then she pivoted and ran to catch up to Harper.

"I guess I was wrong." Eden bent her head to sniff the blue, yellow and white blooms. "They weren't picking them for their mommy."

Eden was more of a mommy to the girls than Lily had ever been.

And it wasn't fair of him to want her to play the part without offering her all she deserved.

Maybe she was right. Nothing could come of their kiss. Even if it had rocked his world and tempted him to offer her everything.

Eden needed to talk to Gabby. Now.

She waited on the porch of the house Dylan and Gabby had moved into after recently getting married. It was a large home with several acres of land and a river snaking around the back of the property.

"Eden? What are you doing here?" Gabby held Phoebe on her hip as she let Eden inside. Phoebe instantly squirmed with both arms held out to Eden. "Looks like someone misses you."

Eden laughed and took Phoebe. "How's my Phoebe-kins? You get to spend the morning with me and the girls tomorrow."

The child wriggled to be let down. Eden held her hand as they went into the living room. Phoebe instantly tod-dled over to the colorful plastic blocks on the floor, while Gabby took a seat on the tan sectional. Gabby's dark hair was pulled back into a ponytail, and she wore black leggings with a blousy red T-shirt.

Eden collapsed on the other end of the sectional.

"What. Is. Going. On?" Gabby asked. "Something's wrong."

"Nothing's wrong." Eden shook her head. "I'm just confused. I need help sorting out my thoughts."

Her friend brightened. "Tell me everything."

Oh, boy. She probably should have thought this through before showing up. But she and Gabby had shared a lot these past years.

"Ryder's ex-wife is coming to town on Friday."

"Lily Haviland? Here?" She let out a small squeal. "Just think. We might get to see her. Remember when we went to see *The Wrong Kind of Right*? She was amazing in it. I wish they made more rom-coms like that."

Eden was taken aback. She thought of Lily less as a movie star and more as Ryder's ex-wife at this point. Not long ago, her own reaction would have been similar to Gabby's. So much had changed since Ryder moved here.

"She *was* great in that movie." Eden tried to figure out where to start. "This isn't about Lily, though."

"Oh?" Gabby tilted her head. "What is it about?"

Ryder kissed me. And I love him. But we can't be to-gether. He doesn't want to get married. Ever. And even if he did, it wouldn't be fair to the twins. They want their mom and dad together, and can you blame them?

"It's kind of hard…" Eden smoothed the edge of her shirt. "It's going to sound dumb."

"Seriously?" Gabby gave her the deadpan stare. "If it's bothering you, it's not dumb."

"I care about the girls. They're so full of life." She wasn't sure how to put in words what she was feeling.

"They are adorable. Phoebe loves them, too. They're like her big sisters."

She thought back to when she'd first asked Gabby if it would be okay for her to babysit all three girls. Her friend had agreed instantly, claiming they'd be like siblings for Phoebe. Gabby had such a big heart.

"They're wound up about Lily coming. Super excited, but nervous, too."

"Oh, poor things. I'm sure it must be hard on them not having her around."

"Yeah, it is. Ivy wants them to get back together."

"Understandable."

"Ryder claims it will never happen."

"Again, understandable."

"He also claims he'll never get remarried."

"I wouldn't be too sure about that." Gabby's self-satisfied grin made Eden's arm hair stand on end. She ran her palms over her arms to ease the sensation.

"I want him to be happy. I want the girls to be happy." Her neck felt warm. "I'm confused."

"Are you attracted to him?" Gabby leaned in. "I know you weren't before…"

"Yes." She stared at the ceiling. "I'm attracted to him. I've always been attracted to him. I just didn't like him before."

"Oh." The word lilted upward in hope.

"No. It's wrong. I can't do that to the girls."

"The girls?" Gabby pulled a face. "What about Ryder? What about you?"

Her heart throbbed at the thought of him. His honesty. His work ethic. His patience. His generosity.

"Eden, maybe this is your chance. How many times over the years did you say you wanted to get married and have a family and live on a ranch and have Christmases in your childhood home? Ryder could offer you all of those things."

Yes, he could. Her lungs squeezed more than she thought possible.

Gabby continued. "But it wouldn't be fair to him if you wanted him only for what he could give you."

She agreed.

"Take away the ranch—your family's ranch—and the twins. Put Ryder all by himself with none of the extras. Would you be interested in him?" Gabby's gaze scared her.

Would she still love Ryder without the girls or the ranch?

Yes. A thousand times over.

But could he ever love her? Enough to rethink his marriage stance?

She didn't know.

And until she did, she had to put these feelings into cold storage. Because her love for Ryder was real, but her love for the girls was, too. And regardless of what was growing between her and Ryder, she couldn't act on it. The twins needed their real mommy now.

Chapter Eleven

"**Y**ou're a fast learner, Ivy." Thursday afternoon, Eden's mom planted a kiss on the girl's head, then held out the tissue-paper flower they'd made. "Now you can have bouquets of flowers anytime you want."

"I'm going to make another one." Ivy raced over to the plastic bag Mom had brought full of assorted colors of tissue paper and other craft items.

Eden locked eyes with her mom, and they both chuckled. Her parents had shown up bright and early at Ryder's, and while Dad was spending the day trotting around the ranch with him, Mom was hanging out with Eden and the twins. Phoebe had been here earlier. Gabby picked her up after lunch and stayed for about an hour before taking off.

Right now Eden could use Mom's moral support. She had a bad feeling that after Lily arrived tomorrow, everything would be different. Between her and Ryder, at least.

One more day... She could enjoy life the way it was for one more day.

Harper carried Dandy over to Mom. "She wants to sit on your lap."

"My lap's plenty big enough for both of you." Mom's lips twitched in amusement.

Harper didn't need to be told twice. She climbed up and rested the back of her head against Mom's chest, trying to hold the squirming kitten.

"It's okay if Dandy wants to get down," Mom said. "You and I can still snuggle."

Harper released the kitten, and Dandy made a clean getaway. The fact the girls liked her mother made Eden happy not just for their sakes, but for Mom's, too. She was a wonderful grandma. She'd spent countless hours with Noah over the years. They had a special bond.

"I'm so happy I could come spend the day with you two." Mom stroked Harper's hair. "Grandpa Bill doesn't always want to do crafts and have tea parties."

Ivy came up to Eden with pink tissue paper in one hand and purple in the other. "What color should I make?"

"How about both?"

"At the same time?" The possibility made her mouth form an O.

"Yes. If we alternate the colors before folding, the flower will have pink *and* purple petals." Eden patted the chair next to her, and they spread out the first layer of pink tissue paper, then topped it with purple and continued alternating until finishing. Ivy folded it the way Eden's mom showed her earlier. "Why don't you make a few more to give to your mother tomorrow?"

"She'll like that." Ivy's blue eyes glimmered like sunshine on a lake. "Grandma Page, our mommy is coming tomorrow."

"Yes, you've mentioned it a time or two." Mom smiled at her. "I think it's wonderful you're taking the time to make special things for her."

Harper twisted her neck to stare up at Mom. "I'm going to show her how I can ride a pony."

"Patches isn't a pony," Ivy muttered.

Harper glared at her sister until she returned her attention to making the flowers. "Daddy said I can wear my new shiny shirt. It's purple and white. It's fancy."

"We made lots of presents for her." Ivy abandoned the tissue paper and raced to the books Eden had finished last night. The girls had helped select the pictures, projects and worksheets to put in each binder. They'd each made a collage of their names on craft paper, and Eden had inserted them into the clear protectors of the binder covers.

"Want to see?" Harper climbed off Mom's lap. "Come on."

The flowerpots and other gifts were in the sunroom with the door closed so the kittens wouldn't destroy them.

"These are works of art." Mom inspected each project lined up on the coffee table and asked questions as she did. The twins were happy to answer her. Sunlight filled the room, and Eden had flashbacks of her and Mia lounging in there, reading or giggling about something from school. This room would always hold good memories.

"Daddy said she'll have to leave the flowerpots here, but we can ship everything else to her if it won't fit on the plane." Harper had one hand on her hip and gestured to the projects with her other hand.

"Mommy will find a way to take the flowerpots home." Ivy stood with her feet together and chin high.

Eden exchanged a glance with Mom. She should have thought that particular gift through better. She'd forgotten about the plane.

"I'm sure she'll want to take them with her," Mom said. "But the airline might not let her."

"We can wrap them in plastic bags, right Harper?" Ivy sounded confident.

Harper shrugged.

"She'll take them," the girl declared again.

"Your mother will have to leave them here, Ivy," Eden said gently. "But you can tell her you'll think about her every time you look at the flowers."

Ivy's cheeks grew splotchy and her eyes filled with tears, but she held herself together.

"Oh, would you look at that?" Eden pretended to check her phone. "Almost four o'clock. It's about time for your favorite cartoon. Why don't you two wash your hands and get comfy on the couch? Mom and I will make you a snack."

"Okay!" They raced out of the room.

"Ivy's a little wound up, huh?" Mom asked.

"Yeah. I've talked to her and tried to be as tender as I can, but I have a bad feeling she's going to be disappointed with this visit. Her expectations are so high."

"Poor thing."

"Harper's on edge, too. She's more realistic, but…both girls could use a long stretch of time with their mother. I'm glad Lily is coming." She was glad for the girls' sake, but for her own? She wouldn't think about it.

"I am, too." Mom led the way out of the room, and Eden closed the doors. "They're both so sweet—I want them to be happy."

"Same here. I'm doing my best." Eden frowned. "I love them. It's going to be hard when summer ends."

"It's not as if you won't ever see them again." They crossed the hall and headed to the kitchen.

"I know, but it won't be the same." Eden knew that firsthand. She'd babysat for Noah until he was almost four years old, and she still spent time with him, but it wasn't as intimate as when they'd spent every day together.

"You'll have other things to focus on. Have you registered for your classes yet?"

"I started to, but one of the classes is full." Eden rummaged through the pantry for juice boxes and pretzels. "I need to talk to an adviser about either getting on a wait-list or switching classes."

"Are you excited?" Mom opened the fridge and found a bag of clementines. She peeled two of them while Eden filled two small bowls with pretzels.

"I will be." She was trying to help the twins prepare for this visit first. "Other things have been distracting me, but I'm sure I'll get more excited as fall approaches."

Mom cast her a sly glance. "I like the things that have been distracting you."

Her and her big mouth.

"Ryder is a wonderful man," Mom said. "Babysitting the girls here has been good for you."

Her mom knew her too well.

"I agree." Eden gave her mom a pointed stare. "But that's all it is. Babysitting."

"I can't help but see God's hand in this. Your dad and I wrestled with selling this place, and when we found out Ryder wanted it, we knew it was an answer to our prayer. It's practically in our family, since Mason is his brother. And buying the RV helped get the restlessness out of your father. He still gets antsy, though. It was nice of Ryder to invite him over today. Your dad misses ranching."

"I'm sure Ryder appreciates Dad helping out."

"Your dad appreciates being included. God knew Ryder and the girls needed you, too."

As much as she'd like to think God had a master plan for her involving Ryder and the girls, her gut told her otherwise.

"Don't get your hopes up, Mom."

"What do you mean?"

Eden took a few steps backward to check on the girls.

They'd turned on the television and were sitting together on the couch. "I mean, I can see where you're going with this. It's not going to happen. Ryder went through a lot with his divorce and doesn't want a commitment again. And the girls have a lot of unresolved issues concerning their mother."

Mom frowned. "I didn't realize." Then she brightened. "God can heal any wound. Anything is possible."

Anything *was* possible, but probable? Not likely.

The doorbell rang. Eden almost jumped. "I'll be right back."

She loped to the hall and opened the front door.

Lily Haviland stood in front of her.

Long waves of silky dark brown hair cascaded over her shoulders. She wore a stylish red blouse, pencil-thin dark jeans that ended at her ankle and red high heels. Her makeup accentuated her piercing blue eyes, the same shade as the twins'.

"Oh, hi," Eden stammered. "We weren't expecting you until tomorrow. Come in."

"I had a break in my schedule and figured I'd get a jump start."

Only then did Eden realize Lily wasn't alone. A full-figured woman in her early thirties stood behind her. Eden ushered them inside and introduced herself.

"Nanny Eden." Lily smiled, revealing perfect white teeth. "The girls have been raving about you." She turned to the other woman. "This is my assistant, Mandy Drake."

Mandy wore black pants and a white shirt and carried a large black tote. Earbuds were in her ears, and she was furiously typing something into her phone. Then she finished and offered her hand. Eden shook it, unsure of what to make of Mandy's no-nonsense persona.

"This is my mom, Joanna Page." Eden flourished her hand toward her mother.

"Oh, my, it's nice to meet you." Mom wiped her hands on a kitchen towel as she stepped forward. "We loved *Courtroom Crimes*. We watched every episode, didn't we, Eden?"

Eden nodded, suddenly embarrassed. The fact she was standing in front of one of her favorite movie stars and babysitting the woman's children hit her in an odd way. She didn't feel in awe of Lily anymore. No, it was more of a feeling of insignificance, like who was she to harbor dreams of forever with this woman's ex-husband and daughters? What a joke.

"Where's Ryder?" Lily asked.

Before Eden could answer, the twins ran into the kitchen. "Mommy, Mommy!" They attached themselves like barnacles around her legs, and she laughed. "There you are. My sweethearts."

"You came! Did you miss us?" Ivy hopped up and down, her face flushed with joy.

"Of course, I missed you!" She hugged them one by one. "That's why I'm here."

"We made you presents!" Ivy dragged her by the hand in the direction of the sunroom. Harper took Lily's other hand.

Even Lily's laugh seemed to be brighter than the average person's. "You did? Aw, thank you."

As the three of them left the kitchen, Mandy looked torn on if she should follow her boss or stay put.

"Would you like to sit down?" Eden belatedly remembered her manners. "We were just getting ready to have a snack. I'll put on a pot of coffee. Mom, where are the muffins you brought?"

"I'd love a muffin and coffee, thanks." Mandy visibly

relaxed, setting the tote bag in the hallway before taking a seat on a stool at the island. "I didn't realize the drive from the airport would take so long."

"The mountains and two-lane roads add on extra time." Mom lifted the lid off a plastic container filled with blueberry muffins. "Here, take one. Or two. We're not shy here."

Mandy selected one as Eden filled the coffeepot. The twins' chipper voices could be heard, along with Lily's voice, from the other room. As Mom made small talk with Mandy, the coffee maker rumbled softly.

Harper yelled something. Then Ivy shouted back. And Eden wondered if she should check on them to intervene.

"Go get your nanny," Lily said loudly. Dead silence weighed oppressively in the air.

Eden excused herself. "I'll see how they're doing."

She went to the sunroom, where Lily spotted her right away. "You did all these crafts with the girls?"

"Yes. They're for you." Eden peeked at Ivy, who seemed subdued, and then Harper, who scooted closer to Ivy and took her hand in hers. "The girls wanted to make you presents. They are so thoughtful."

The sight of those two darling children holding hands, supporting each other, tore at her heart. Eden would do anything to make this visit go well for them, and they both looked like they were struggling at the moment.

"Ivy took extra care with the necklace. She dyed the noodles hot pink and picked the best noodles for it. She thought you'd like pink the best." Eden smiled at Ivy. "And Harper spent hours making the mosaic butterfly out of gem stickers. She's drawn to nature. They're very talented."

"I see that," Lily said softly.

Eden hoped so. *God, please let Lily see how much her daughters need her.*

"Oh, girls, why don't you go get your books?" Eden asked brightly. "You can show them to your mom."

"You can show them to me later," Lily said to the twins. "I need to talk to your father first." She addressed Eden. "When do you expect him back?"

"Um, it depends. Between five and six, I guess."

Lily swiped her phone and typed into it. When she finished, she smiled broadly. "There. He's on his way."

Ryder about dropped his phone when he read Lily's text. She was here? Now? So much for arriving tomorrow evening. He clenched his jaw and turned to Bill. They'd finished taking care of the horses and were reviewing Ryder's to-do list in his ranch office.

"Looks like I've got to wrap this up. Lily's here."

"Oh?" Bill took off his cowboy hat and wiped his forehead, then put it back on. "I thought she was coming tomorrow."

"So did I." He wasn't prepared to deal with her yet. His muscles tensed as he realized his ex-wife was at the house now saying who knew what to Eden and her mom.

His stomach clenched. Lily had a knack for being nice to people and playing the perfect mommy role. But she could keep it up for only a limited period before she cracked. He didn't want the girls to be on the brunt end of her dismissal—not on day one, at least.

"I really appreciate you spending the day with me, Bill." Ryder led the way outside where the sunshine made the grass a little greener and the sky a little bluer. "I wish you were around more often. I could use a master rancher like you teaching me."

Bill guffawed. "Master? I don't know about that. Just

years and years of experience. The place grows on you, and it takes time. But if we lived around here, I'd take you up on it. I miss riding out and checking cattle. I even miss checking fence, and I never thought I'd say those words."

"Anytime you're in town, come over. You're always welcome. In fact, you're more than welcome."

"I appreciate it, Ryder." His voice was gravelly. "You're doing a good job here."

"That's kind of you to say." The praise lifted his spirits, but he was well aware of all the ways he didn't measure up.

"I wasn't saying it just to say it." Bill gave him a shrewd sideways glance. "You've got good instincts, and the improvements you're considering will bring in extra revenue in the long run. Ranching isn't only about knowing cattle—it's a business, son, and you've got the head for it."

A sudden rush of emotion hit him, but he'd tuck the words aside to enjoy later. The side door to the house was a few feet away, and he had his ex-wife to contend with.

He opened the door for Bill, and they took turns washing up before entering the kitchen.

Ryder took in the scene like a snapshot. Lily sat on a stool at the island with Ivy and Harper on either side, their stools as close to hers as they could possibly get them. Mandy was making small talk with Eden as Eden poured coffee. Joanna was watching Lily and the girls with a puzzled expression on her face.

Lily's phone rang, and she stood and raised her finger to the girls, her face aglow. "Sam? Yes…" She left the room, her heels clicking across the hardwood floor.

The twins noticed him then. "Daddy! Mommy came early and she loves her presents…"

"What a good surprise, huh?" He kept his tone upbeat

for their sake. Personally, he wished she had arrived when she'd said she would.

"We'll get out of here." Joanna crossed over and gave Ryder a hug. "I'm sure you want some family time."

Eden startled. "Oh, yes, I'm leaving, too. It was nice to meet you, Mandy."

"Yes, nice to meet you. Delicious muffins, Joanna." Mandy hitched her thumb toward where Lily had disappeared. "I'll just get some air…"

Normally, Ryder would ask them all to stay, but this visit would be best done alone. The girls deserved uninterrupted time with their mother.

He followed them all to the door and held it open for them to leave. The twins stood in front of him, waving and saying their goodbyes. He sensed Lily come up behind him, and she called out goodbye, too. He tried to meet Eden's eyes, but her glance back lasted only a split second.

A large black SUV with tinted windows was parked outside. Lily's security detail, most likely.

With the Pages gone, he closed the door and straightened his spine. "Hello, Lily."

"Ryder." She tilted her head as her features transformed to her wide-eyed, I-have-bad-news-but-am-totally-not-to-blame expression. He'd seen it many times. His temples started to throb. She smiled. "You look good."

"You, too." He willed himself not to clench his jaw. "A little surprised to see you. Thought you were arriving tomorrow night."

"There was an unexpected break in my schedule."

The twins were watching them in silence.

"Where's Mandy?" he asked.

"She needed to make some calls. She's hanging out

with Andre." Lily pointed to the door. He figured Andre was in the SUV.

"She's welcome to stay inside."

"That's okay."

"Well, why don't we go to the living room." He extended his arm. The girls skipped ahead and sat on the couch, patting it for Lily to sit with them, which she did. He eased his aching joints into the chair across from them. "We're glad you could come."

A calculated look flitted through her eyes. If he didn't know her better, he'd convince himself he was imagining it. But he did know her.

It was another sign that unpleasant news was pending.

He wanted to sigh and run his fingers through his hair, but he needed to keep up a strong front for the girls. Whatever bad news Lily was about to share would be best heard alone.

"Harper, Ivy, can you give your mother and me a few minutes to talk? Why don't you play with the kittens in one of your rooms for a little bit?"

"But Daddy..." Ivy whined.

"I know," he said. "You'll see lots of Mommy, don't worry. Just for a bit, okay?"

"Yes, Daddy." They slid off the couch and meekly trudged upstairs.

"What's going on?" he asked when the coast was clear.

"What do you mean?" She crossed one leg over the other. The red stilettos reminded him of sharp, bloody weapons.

Usually this would be the time he goaded her into an argument about arriving early without warning him, but he could tell something was off. And a sense of calm permeated his body as he studied the stunning woman he'd once loved.

He didn't feel an ounce of anything for her anymore. Not anger. Not love. Not guilt.

The silence stretched until her chin rose. "I do have some news, actually."

"Oh?" He prepared himself for the announcement of a three-movie deal with extensive worldwide travel. Or she'd landed a series and would be working sixteen-hour days all summer. Maybe she was moving to France. Who knew? He was used to it, and for the first time it evoked no reaction from him.

"Sam and I…" She averted her eyes, her thumb and index finger rubbing together in a nervous tic. "This isn't… I don't know why this is so hard…"

Uncertainty pooled in his gut. Who was Sam?

"We're getting married."

A strange sensation spread through his body. She was getting married. To Sam. But he didn't know a Sam. She'd moved in with Derrick when she left him.

"Who's Sam?" He was surprised his voice sounded so normal.

"Sam Pendleton. The producer of *Shimmy Lies*." She made it sound as if everyone knew Sam Pendleton. Everyone in Hollywood probably did. He'd stopped caring about that scene long ago.

So she was getting married. He supposed he should be upset, but he wasn't. He didn't know what he felt. Maybe nothing at all.

"Okay." He leaned back in his chair.

Two tiny wrinkles appeared above the bridge of her nose. "That's all you're going to say? Okay?"

"Congratulations?" What did she want from him?

Her tongue worked over her teeth under her tightly closed lips. "We haven't set a date yet, and naturally, we'll be keeping it a tight secret for security reasons. The twins will be flower girls."

The twins. His heart dropped. While the idea of her getting remarried didn't bother him, it would definitely bother the girls.

"After you tell them—" she'd adopted her sweet, innocent persona, the one he'd fallen in love with way back when "—I'll send my stylist out here with dress samples and to have them fitted."

Now he understood the previous glint in her eye. It wasn't because she'd worried about his reaction to her news.

She didn't want to tell the girls she was getting remarried.

She wanted him to do it.

She expected him to do her dirty work.

"The stylist is fine with me." He shrugged, keeping his cool. "But you have to tell the girls yourself. They need to hear it from you."

"Me?" She stood, fanning herself, and began to pace. "But Ryder, you're with them all the time. They'll take it better from you."

"Lily, they've been bouncing off the walls all week they've been so excited to see you. I can't be everything for them."

"Everything?" She gave him a look that said *get real*. "Don't be dramatic. You're out all day living out some cowboy fantasy. Nanny Eden is spending all the time with them."

"It's not Nanny Eden," he said through clenched teeth. "It's Auntie Eden, and she isn't the nanny. She's a good friend of mine who is doing me—doing us—a favor."

"Well, if she's such a good friend, maybe the girls would take the news better from her."

His jaw dropped. Had she really just suggested that Eden tell the girls about her upcoming nuptials?

Selfish. She's unbelievably selfish. What did I ever see in her?

The familiar anger and resentment started building steam within him. He curled his fingers into his palms. *Let it go. Don't get worked up. She's not worth it.*

He took a deep breath. "Lily, they need to hear it from you."

"Why? What's the big deal?" She tossed her hair. The motion was all bravado. Her eyes revealed her fear. "They'll adore Sam. He has three kids, too."

Three kids? Ugh. The girls would have stepsiblings. And who knew how they were being raised. Would Lily start wanting to have regular visitations? Would she expect the girls to be best friends with their new stepbrothers and stepsisters?

"His kids are older, of course." Lily flicked her fingernails. "His youngest is in college."

He wasn't entirely sure why he was so relieved to hear it.

"This all happened quickly. Sam wanted to put a ring on it." She pointed to the gigantic engagement ring Ryder hadn't noticed until now. Then she sat again, letting her forehead drop into her hands. "Of course I had to say yes, but I didn't realize how hard all this would be."

Of course she had to say yes? What an odd phrase. And that was when it hit him. She was already looking for a way out of the engagement. Just like she'd gotten out of their marriage and how she continually shirked her duty to the girls.

He saw her clearly, maybe for the first time.

Lily hadn't left him because of something he did or who he was.

She'd left him because she couldn't handle commitment.

Pity for her swept through him. To the outside world, Lily had it all. But he knew the truth—she rejected what really mattered. She was missing out on the most important things in life.

He went over and sat beside her.

"You don't have to marry him, Lily, but I don't think this is about him."

"You don't?" She glanced up at him.

"Do you love him?"

"Yes, I do."

"Then give him a chance. Be honest with him. Don't walk away from him the way you did me."

As his words sank in, her face fell.

"If you need moral support telling Harper and Ivy about getting remarried, I'll be right there with you. Do you want to tell them now? Or do you want to wait until next week before you leave?"

"About that…" She had the grace to flush.

He didn't even get irritated. He knew her well enough to know she'd never planned on staying an entire week. It had sounded good. Something a caring mother would do. And for Lily, words were more important than actions.

"I'm heading out tomorrow night." She flashed him a quick look. "I have rehearsals…"

Instead of railing at her or giving her the silent treatment or even pleading with her to change her mind, he simply nodded. "Then I guess we'd better make the most of your visit. I'll get the girls. You might as well tell them now."

He stood and turned in the direction of the stairs. Tonight was going to be rough on the twins. But his heart grew lighter with each step.

He finally had peace about his marriage and divorce.

Lily couldn't handle being perceived as anything but America's sweetheart. Telling him one thing and doing another was her way of convincing herself good intentions were enough.

He'd married her thinking he didn't deserve her. But now he understood the truth—she didn't deserve him.

Ryder paused in the doorway of Ivy's room, where the girls sat on the floor whispering.

"Why don't you two come downstairs?" He smiled at them. "Your mother has something to tell you."

Gone was their joyful exuberance. Gone was their excitement about seeing their mother. They both stood. Ivy reached for his left hand, and Harper reached for his right. Together, they walked down to the living room.

Please, Lord God, help me comfort them when Lily breaks it to them.

He wished Eden was here. She'd know how to soothe them. She'd know what to say.

God, I need her. I need Eden. Not just for the summer. Not just for the girls.

When Lily's visit was over, he was going to figure out how to tell Eden the truth.

He needed her. Forever.

Chapter Twelve

"I was surprised at how often Lily checked her phone," Eden's mother said as she poked her fork into the mound of mashed potatoes and gravy on her plate. Dad sat next to her, attacking his order of meat loaf with gusto. Eden and her parents had driven to Riverview Lounge after leaving Ryder's place.

"I'm sure she's busy." Eden hadn't really noticed. She'd been lost in her own little world—a world that had seemed to shrink the instant Lily appeared in her fabulous red shoes, stylish outfit and perfect hair.

The fantasy was officially over.

"I didn't like how she referred to you as the nanny, and she wasn't there five minutes before she took a phone call. Didn't she notice how excited the girls were to see her?" Mom patted her lips with her napkin and shook her head. "All that work you put into those gifts and books—and she said the right things, but it was like her heart wasn't in it."

"It's okay, Mom. She'll be here for a week. It's not fair to judge her for being distracted for ten minutes." All Eden could picture was the four of them—Ryder with

Lily next to him and the twins in front of them—waving
and calling goodbye from the front porch.

The perfect family.

Eden lost what little appetite she had.

"Ryder's doing a good job with the ranch." Dad paused
to take a sip of iced tea. "He told me I can stop by anytime."

"That's nice of him. He's so thoughtful." Mom patted Dad's arm.

"I don't think he was just saying it, either." Dad looked
serious.

"I'm sure he wasn't." Eden found it easy to reassure
her father. "You could teach him a thing or two about
raising cattle in Rendezvous."

His face brightened. "I wouldn't mind." He shot
a quick glance at her mom. "When we're in town, of
course."

"If Ryder doesn't mind you riding out with him now
and again, we might have to park here more often." Mom
gave him an understanding smile. "I know you miss it."

Warning flags started popping up in Eden's mind.

She wasn't the only one losing her heart to Ryder and
the girls. Her parents were, too.

How had she missed it? Her mom treated Harper
and Ivy like they were her own granddaughters. And
in Mom's eyes, the sun rose and set on their daddy. And
what about Dad? He acted like he'd been thrown a life-
line because Ryder wanted him to hang out at the ranch.

Eden should have seen it coming. All three of them
craved a familiar life with their ranch at the heart of it.
But they weren't being fair to Ryder.

"I'm sorry to do this, but I've got to go." She covered
her half-eaten bowl of minestrone with a napkin, grabbed
her purse and scooted out of the booth.

"You sick? I'll drive you home." Dad sprang to his feet.

"No, no. You two stay here. I'll walk. It's not far." She dragged her finger across her eyebrow. "I just need to think. I'll see you tomorrow."

Her parents exchanged glances, but they let her walk away.

She weaved through the busy restaurant until she made it outside. A picture-perfect summer evening greeted her as she turned left and headed to her apartment.

The warm air couldn't penetrate the chill over her heart. She'd been an idiot, letting herself fall in love with Ryder. The girls, well, she'd loved them from the day she'd met them. That couldn't have been prevented. But Ryder? She could have—should have—done a lot of things differently.

He had enough problems. He didn't want the complications love brought, and Eden finally understood why. Lily wasn't just a movie star or his ex-wife. She was the mother of his children. He would be dealing with her the rest of his life.

Eden tried to swallow the lump forming in her throat. The memory of his arms around her roared back. His lips on hers had been the best thing she'd ever experienced. He'd made her feel safe, cherished, desirable. She'd never felt that way before.

Her phone chirped. A text came through from Ryder. You don't have to come over tomorrow. I'll see you on Monday.

The words hit her like a punch in the stomach. Just as she'd thought. He'd taken one look at Lily and forgotten Eden existed. She was just the babysitter. Nothing more.

She was used to it.

She might as well accept it and move on. Everyone else seemed to be good at going forward. Everyone except her.

* * *

"Come give Mommy a hug goodbye." Lily was likely to topple over as she crouched in the foyer in a pair of pink stilettos Friday afternoon with her arms spread wide. Ryder wanted to roll his eyes.

Harper hugged her willingly. Ivy hung back, a stony expression on her face.

"Now, Ivy, I'm not going to see you for a long time." Lily pretended to pout, but Ivy didn't budge. Lily straightened and tapped her chin. "If I don't get a hug, you might not be a flower girl."

Ryder let his head fall back in exasperation as he gazed at the ceiling and ground his teeth together. Why was she so clueless when it came to her own children? Hadn't Ivy's tears last night when Lily broke her news about getting married clued her in that the girls could not care less about being in her wedding?

"I don't want to be a flower girl!" Ivy shouted, turning and racing upstairs. Harper quickly followed.

Lily gaped at him. "And how am I supposed to respond to that?"

She acted like Ivy was to blame. Ryder narrowed his eyes. "You can't expect them to be overjoyed at your news."

"Why not? Not every little girl gets to wear a custom-designed dress to her mother's wedding. It will be an exclusive event. They should be happy."

"They're five. They don't even understand that you're a movie star."

"Great." Lily pulled her sunglasses out of her oversize purse and set them on her head. "I don't have time for this."

"Maybe you should make the time."

"Look, I'm not going to be held hostage by those two."

"They're your daughters, not dolls to dress up. They have feelings, Lily."

"I know that, Ryder," she said with an abundance of sarcasm. "What about my feelings? Shouldn't they be glad I'm getting married?"

Don't react. Do not react.

"I've got to go." She flourished her hand to the door. "Tell them bye for me."

"Will you wait five minutes?" he asked. She was really going to leave without attempting to soothe their feelings? The woman had hit a new low in his book. "Go up and talk to them. For crying out loud, this isn't the time to leave."

"Fine." Her tone could have sliced through metal. She click-clacked down the hall and went upstairs. He followed at a distance and waited in the doorway while she went into Ivy's room.

"Why don't you want to be a flower girl?" Lily asked brusquely. "Don't you want a pretty dress?"

Ryder peeked through the doorway. Ivy had her back to Lily.

"It's not the dress," Harper said. She snuck a glance at Ivy, still ignoring her mother.

"What is it, then?"

"Harper," Ivy warned.

Harper's glance darted back and forth to Ivy and Lily.

"You can tell me." Lily nodded encouragingly.

"You tell her, Ivy." Harper closed the distance to her twin and took her hand in hers. "Go ahead."

"I don't want you to marry him." Ivy faced Lily then, with tear marks racing down her cheeks. "Why aren't you marrying Daddy?"

"You haven't even met Sam. And as for Daddy, no."

Lily let out a strangled laugh. "We're not getting married again."

"But why not?" Ivy inched closer to her. "Daddy's so handsome."

"Well, of course he is," Lily said. "But I love someone else now."

"What if we moved back to California?" Ivy tipped her head slightly to look up at Lily. "Then you'd see Daddy lots, and we'd all be together. We could live in the same house."

Ryder held his breath. *Come on, Lily, tell her the truth. Don't tell her what she wants to hear because it will be easier for you.*

"I'd love it if you moved back to California."

He closed his eyes, dread lashing at him like a winter storm.

"But we're not all going to live together again. I'm marrying Sam."

The relief was so sudden he propped his hand against the doorjamb to keep his balance.

"I don't want you to marry Sam!" Ivy stamped her foot. "I want you to marry Daddy!"

"That's enough, Ivy. I'm marrying Sam, and I don't need your permission." Lily straightened. "Now I have to go. It's your last chance for a hug."

Ivy turned her back to her once more.

"Okay. It's your choice. Bye."

Lily breezed past Ryder, down the hall to the stairs. He debated following her. He could hear her heels clicking as Ivy ran out of the room, yelling, "Mommy!"

She sobbed all the way down the stairs, hysterically yelling for her mother. Ryder and Harper followed close behind. He hated seeing her so upset. Wished this all could have worked out differently. How? He had no clue.

He just hated that the divorce had caused so much pain. Still caused so much pain.

At the bottom of the staircase, he stopped short. Lily held Ivy in her arms as Ivy sobbed.

"I'll always love you, you know. It's just… Daddy and I aren't getting back together. Ever." Lily met his eyes, and he nodded in thanks. Then she set Ivy back on her feet. "Now be good, okay?"

Ivy sniffled and nodded.

Lily waved to them and walked out the door. As the screen door shut, Ivy pressed her little hands against it and watched her go.

"Come on." Ryder reached out to touch her shoulder, and she launched herself into his arms. He picked her up and held her tightly. "It'll be okay."

Ivy started crying again, and Harper glued herself to his side. He held her hand, leading her to the living room, where they all smooshed together on the couch.

"I'm sorry." He looked down at Harper and at Ivy. "I know you're both disappointed. This wasn't how you wanted the visit to go. You were hoping to have Mommy all week, and instead you found out some tough news, and your time was cut short."

"Mommy never stays more than a day." Harper sounded matter-of-fact, but her lower lip wobbled.

"At least you had her for a little while." He pulled her closer. "And I don't blame either of you for wanting us to get back together. That's normal."

Ivy lifted waterlogged eyes to him and wiped the back of her hand under her nose.

"You can talk to me about anything, okay?" he said. "I'm always here for you. I'm always going to be here for you."

Harper hugged his arm and kissed his biceps. "I love you, Daddy."

"I love you, too."

Ivy looked crushed. He kissed the top of her head. "I'm sorry, Ivy. I know you're really disappointed."

She seemed at a loss for words. He had a feeling this was one of those events where only time would heal her. He couldn't rush it.

He thought about his own wounds and how time had healed them.

Ever since meeting Eden, he'd been trying to convince himself he couldn't have a future with her—or with any woman. He'd been wrong.

Eden had opened his eyes to what real love, a lasting partnership, could be.

And he wanted it. The connection, the commitment, the peace deep down that he could always count on her.

But did she feel the same?

Saturday morning Eden printed out the courses she'd signed up for. Too bad she felt zero enthusiasm about them. She wanted more than a career. She wanted Ryder. The girls. The ranch.

As usual, she wanted it all.

She'd slept poorly with bad dreams. Every one of them involved her being paralyzed or not being able to speak while trying to warn someone of danger.

Mom and Dad had stopped by yesterday and called earlier this morning to check on her, and she'd assured them she was fine and shooed them out of the apartment. Thankfully, they were spending a few days at the hot springs a county over with friends.

A knock on the door lured her to the hall. Eden opened

the door. Ryder, freshly showered from the looks of it, stood before her with brooding eyes. Her mouth went dry.

"What are you doing here?" she asked. "I thought you didn't need me this weekend."

"The ranch hands agreed to handle the chores so I could be with the girls." He sighed. "Lily left last night." He didn't seem upset about it.

"Already? Are the girls okay? Ivy?" She hated to think of poor Ivy distraught. Harper, too, but Ivy had built up this visit so much in her mind.

"She was upset, but they're both coming around. Can I come in?" He shifted his weight from one foot to the other.

"I don't think that's a good idea."

"Why not?"

Because all I want to do is wrap my arms around you. But you don't want a relationship. And I'm not the one for you even if you did.

"Please?" He looked so sincere that she caved, held the door open and moved aside to let him in.

They went to the living room. She sat on the couch and waited for him to settle in a chair.

"Lily's getting married."

Married? She sucked in a breath. Ivy would be crushed. Harper, too. Her already low spirits plummeted. "Oh, no."

"She told me as soon as you all left the other night. The twins were pretty upset, but Ivy took it the worst."

"I'm sorry, Ryder."

"Don't be. It was inevitable. And it has nothing to do with you…"

He was right. It didn't have anything to do with her. But she wanted it to—she wanted so badly to be part of their lives. Not as the babysitter, and not as a bystander.

"I think Ivy's starting to accept it," he said.

"And Harper?"

"Has a more realistic view of her mother than Ivy does."

Eden silently agreed.

"I'm glad she came," Ryder said. "And I'm glad she's getting married, and I'm glad she left early."

Eden frowned. What was he getting at?

"I finally realized something, Eden." He stared at her then, and his gaze was hot, intense. "I'm ready to move on, too."

She wasn't sure what to say. It seemed sudden.

"You and I have grown close—don't try to deny it. I admire your devotion to the girls. I like being with you. I trust you. I want to explore this—" he pointed his fingers to her, then back to himself "—whatever this is between us."

Her mind went haywire. He didn't mean it. Couldn't mean it.

This was too easy.

And too convenient.

Lily had barely left.

He was hurting. Not thinking straight. Shocked by his ex's news.

"I think you're confused." She tried to be gentle. "Lily is getting married, and it brought up a lot of emotions for you, I get it. But you don't want this. You don't want me."

"You're wrong." His jaw clenched.

"Ryder, you've been clear that you aren't getting married again. Now your ex-wife comes to town—your glamorous, movie star of an ex-wife—tells you she's getting married, and all of a sudden you want to *explore* whatever is between us? I don't buy it."

"There's nothing to buy, Eden. What about our kiss?"

"It was a kiss." She shot to her feet and turned away. A great kiss. An unbelievable kiss. "Give this a few days, and you'll see I'm right. This is a reaction to Lily's announcement, nothing more."

Ryder gaped at her. Her cheeks were drawn. Her eyes sincere. Did she really think he'd come here as some sort of rebound move?

"It's not a reaction, Eden. I care about you. I have feelings for you."

She shook her head.

"Look me in the eye and tell me you don't have feelings for me, too." He stood and in two strides was in front of her. She looked up at him, and her beautiful brown eyes swam with uncertainty. He waited to hear her say it. But she didn't.

He deserved this, he supposed. He'd barged his way into her life over and over since meeting her. Coming here had been dumb. He shouldn't have pressured her. Something—someone—had ruined love for her.

"Spending time with you… I know you feel it, too." Ryder kept his tone low. "Why won't you tell me the truth? Did someone break your heart? Is that why you won't take a chance on me?"

Her eyes darted back and forth like a caged animal. She looked positively queasy. But then she tilted her chin up a fraction and met his eyes.

"You want the truth?" The words were sharp.

He braced himself, not sure he wanted it anymore.

"The past five years broke my heart."

"Is this about your sister?"

"Partially." She shook her head. "Look, I do have feelings for you. I think you're an amazing father. You care about the ranch. You work hard to protect the cattle. Dad was right to sell it to you. You're fun to be with. Adventurous. I like that you ask for my opinion and actually listen to me."

His mind scrambled to capture each word and lock it inside so he could remember it all later.

"But I also think you're reacting to Lily's visit and her getting engaged. I mean, be real, Ryder. You can't possibly want to date me."

"Why not?" What was she seeing that he wasn't?

"I'm not your type." She widened her eyes to emphasize her point.

"Says who?"

"Says the entire free world." She pointed to the hall. "It's best if we pretend this conversation never happened. You'll wake up tomorrow or next week and be relieved I saw the truth. We never have to talk about it again."

Was he imagining the tremble in her lips? The pain in her eyes?

What did she see when she looked at him? A desperate single dad, hungry for love, glomming on to the babysitter of his kids out of some weird reaction to his famous ex-wife's announcement she was getting remarried?

Maybe she was right.

The image embarrassed him.

"If that's what you want." He held his breath, willing her to change her mind.

"It's for the best."

And with that, an iron door slammed over his heart.

Ironic.

He'd been so adamant about not wanting to get involved again, and the one woman he'd fallen for had taken him at his word.

Ryder cast one more look at her, then stalked down the hall and out the door.

Rejection was one thing he'd learned early on in life. No one ever wanted him for keeps.

Chapter Thirteen

Eden pressed her forehead against the door and slowly turned the dead bolt to lock it. He could give her everything she wanted.

Stop imagining it could have been different.

Too many hopes had gone up in flames over the years.

She'd done the right thing. Ryder would wake up in a few days, and he'd be grateful she'd been the voice of reason. And she'd continue to babysit the girls, albeit with a lump in her throat. She'd avoid him. Bury herself in college plans and helping out her friends—anything to ease the pain of loving Ryder Fanning and knowing he'd never be hers.

He was an honorable man. She'd been honest with him—to a point. She hadn't told him she loved him. She hadn't told him how much he meant to her or how close the girls were to her heart. She would never let him know how tempting he and everything he could offer her were.

Ryder was the one man who could fulfill her dreams.

A husband. Children. Right here in Rendezvous. Living on the ranch, the only home she'd ever known.

She hadn't told him any of those things because it would have trapped him.

It wasn't fair to prey on his confusion right now. Not to him, and not to her, either. Because she didn't want a husband or kids or the ranch if it meant not having his complete devotion.

Without true love, she'd never be happy. The dream would merely be a mirage.

Eden padded to her bedroom and sprawled out on her bed. It had been foolish to fall in love with him and to get so close to the girls.

Another disappointing end in a long string of private heartbreaks.

She'd tossed aside her college plans to come home and be with Mia.

She'd begged the Lord to let Mia live, yet she'd died.

She'd been like a mother to Noah after Mia's death, then Mason had remarried and her services were no longer needed.

She'd spent the bulk of her days caring for baby Phoebe when Gabby had been thrust into motherhood unexpectedly. Then Gabby got married, and those precious days with Phoebe had dwindled to a few hours a week.

It didn't take a genius to see the writing on the wall in her current situation. She'd been given the summer with the girls. After that, the arrangement would be over. And no matter what Ryder said, it would take only a week, tops, for him to realize he wasn't really interested in her.

But…

What if she was wrong?

What if Ryder did have feelings for her and she'd just kicked him out?

Sheer panic shot through her brain.

No, it wasn't possible.

There wasn't a guy in this county who'd shown an ounce of interest in her in years—years! Ryder Fanning—

the gorgeous, intelligent man who wasn't afraid to take risks or ask for help—surely hadn't seen something in her no one else had.

She'd babysit the girls and stay away from him as much as possible.

Tears spilled down her cheeks, because just once in her life she wanted to be wrong. She wanted him to love her. Forever.

"You look like ten miles of dirt road."

Ryder arched his eyebrows at Mason as he stood on his porch. He'd headed directly here after leaving Eden's. He could hear the girls' voices mingling with Noah's from somewhere in the house.

"Want to talk about it?" Mason asked.

He'd planned on picking up the twins, driving back to the ranch and wallowing in rejection all day, but looking at his brother, he realized he *did* want to talk about it.

"Not in there."

"Let's take a walk." Mason gestured toward the out-buildings down the lane.

It was a beautiful day. An eagle flew overhead. Sunshine poured out of the blue skies. But the scene could have been in black and gray for all he cared. Life stank.

They'd made it halfway to the first barn before Ryder could figure out where to start with his messed-up life.

"Did someone break Eden's heart?" The words were out before he could think them through.

Mason squinted, giving him a confused glance. "I don't know, why?"

"Just wondering."

"I mean…" Mason rubbed his chin, looking straight ahead. "I can't think of anyone offhand." He exhaled and shook his head. "I tell you what, I can't even think of the last guy she dated."

A ray of hope lit his heart.

"I'm sure she must have dated in college, but unless she kept it a secret, she hasn't gone out with anyone around here that I can remember, and she's been back for over five years."

"Really?" Ryder frowned. "Are the guys around here stupid or something?"

Mason guffawed. "You have a point. Eden's pretty special."

He wouldn't argue with that.

"The thing about Eden, though… She's quiet. Serious." Mason kept an easy pace. "In some ways, she's easy to overlook. I guess you could say she's in the shadows."

In the shadows? Why? Ever since he'd met her, he'd gravitated to her. Every barbecue, every get-together—all he'd been able to see was Eden.

"I don't get it. Why isn't she married? She's…" Beautiful, real, trustworthy. "She's amazing with kids."

"I know. She was basically Noah's surrogate mom for the first three years of his life. I don't know what I would have done without her."

"And you never considered…" Ryder felt funny bringing this up. "That is…you were never attracted to her?"

Mason pulled a face. "No. I mean, I appreciate her friendship and could see how great she was with Noah, but I wasn't in a mental place to have those kinds of thoughts. And I never got that vibe from her, either."

Eden's declaration about not being attracted to someone who looked like her brother-in-law echoed back. But the weeks had changed her. She hadn't been disgusted by his kiss. Not at all. Warmth pooled all the way to his toes just thinking about it.

"Why all these questions about Eden?" Mason asked. "I thought you were upset about Lily getting remarried."

Why did everyone assume Lily's plans meant anything to him?

"I'm not upset about it." He honestly wasn't. "It's taken some time, but I understand our divorce wasn't really about me. Maybe our marriage wasn't, either. I've made peace with it. I feel bad for the girls. Ivy, especially, has put her mom on a pedestal higher than the Empire State Building."

"For what it's worth, she's been okay today." Mason glanced at him. "She spent some time talking with Brittany while Noah and Harper played tag, but they asked her to play pirates with them, and she ran off with a big smile on her face."

"Good." They reached a split-rail fence. Ryder propped his boot on the bottom rail and looked out over the beautiful land. "I think I'm in love with Eden."

"What?" Mason turned to face him. Ryder just nodded.

"I know. I wasn't prepared for it, either, but I am. I might have started falling for her that day at Christmas Fest. Do you remember? You and I had met, what, a few weeks prior?"

"Yeah, I remember. That was the day Brittany told me it was okay to remember the good times I had with Mia. We were all ice-skating."

"And Lily called while Eden and I were skating with the girls. Eden tore into me after she heard us arguing over the phone in front of the twins."

"Eden always puts kids first." Mason shrugged.

"I think it's one of the reasons I love her. Lily has never put them first. Not one day in her life."

Mason let out a humph. "I love you, Ryder. You know that, right?"

His throat tightened as he nodded.

"But Eden deserves more. If you think you love her only because she'll be a good mom to the twins, well, that's kind of selfish."

Selfish? How could Mason even suggest it?

"Take the twins out of the equation." Mason opened his hands. "Would you still love her?"

"Are you kidding me?" His blood started simmering. "For you to suggest I have feelings for her because I'm looking for a mom for my girls is insulting. And coming from you, it's pretty rich."

Mason looked taken aback. "What do you mean coming from me?"

"Yeah, you." Ryder pointed to him. "Eden practically raised Noah, and then you got married, and it was, 'Oh, by the way, we don't need your services anymore.' Gabby, too. I mean, I get it—they're your kids, not hers. But she put her life on hold to raise your son and Phoebe when you guys needed her. And where did it get her?"

Mason's jaw dropped.

"Eden's more than a babysitter." The fire in Ryder's blood boiled. "She's beautiful. And smart. And she knows the ranch inside and out. She's patient. She sees when I need cheering up and always has the right thing to say. She's got more energy than anyone I know. Do you have any idea how much time she spends planning projects and activities for the girls? I've gone through a dozen nannies—none of them did a fraction of what she does. So, no, I'm not in love with her because I want a mom for the girls, but I do admire how great she is with them."

Mason opened his mouth to speak, but Ryder wasn't finished.

"She deserves more. From all of us. How many nights does Eden babysit Noah even now? I doubt she accepts any pay, either."

Mason clamped his mouth shut.

"So don't ever stand there and give me a lecture about loving her." Ryder jabbed his finger into Mason's chest. "Look in the mirror, bro."

He should have controlled his temper. He inhaled deeply and waited for Mason to start yelling. This was his brother, the man who'd generously taught him the basics of ranching, who'd invited him into his home countless times since they met. He shouldn't have accused him of all those things.

"You're not wrong." Mason hung his head.

Wait...what?

"I never even thought about it, but you're right. I've taken her for granted. Did she say something?"

"No, man. It wouldn't even occur to her." His shoulders slumped. "She loves Noah. Wants to spend time with him. You know how she is."

"Yes, I do." Mason was subdued. "And you're right. She deserves more from me. More from all of us."

"I'm sorry." Ryder felt lower than a grass snake. "I shouldn't have said all that. Honestly, I've never even thought any of it until just now."

"Because you love her. And things get clear when you realize something like that."

"I guess they do."

They turned to stare over the fence at the meadow once more.

It didn't matter if he loved her. Didn't matter if he wanted the world to appreciate her the way he did. She wasn't willing to take him seriously, and he had no one to blame but himself.

* * *

Two hours later, Eden trudged up the hill, indifferent to the beauty of her special place. It wasn't that she didn't notice how the sun brought out the luster of the grass and wildflowers. She was aware of the prairie dogs chasing each other in the distance and the hawk perched on top of a dead tree trunk as it watched for its next meal. Life continued around her, but hers had hit the pause button.

When she reached the flat area, she spread out a quilt and sat cross-legged.

She couldn't shake the feeling she'd made a huge mistake. That she was in the wrong. That she'd miscalculated, violated something precious by sending Ryder on his way.

Sighing, she eased back. The image of Ryder with Lily and the twins waving from their doorway wouldn't let her go. Lily's elegant beauty, her glowing presence had been a shock. She was even more beautiful in person than on-screen. And she hadn't been a diva. Who cared if she'd called Eden the nanny? Technically she was the nanny. Sure, Lily had checked her phone a lot, but she'd been warm to the girls.

Eden hoped Ivy was okay. She wanted to text Ryder and check, but…she couldn't. Ivy had pinned so many hopes on the visit, and finding out her mother was marrying someone else must have been a blow.

She wanted to tuck each girl against her sides, put her arms around them and tell them not to worry, they were loved, that she would always be there for them.

But was it true?

Soon they'd be in school full-time, and she wouldn't see them as much. She would no longer be an important part of their lives, just like she was less and less important to Noah and, to some extent, Phoebe.

It was the way it should be. She wasn't their mother. She'd been blessed to help each one of those children during a critical time in their lives.

Ryder would move on. His heart seemed to be in a better place already. He'd date again. Maybe get married. Misty Sandpiper was more his type. Pretty, put together, bubbly, outgoing. The girls liked her.

A puffy cloud passed overhead, dimming the sunlight. She felt tired. She couldn't remember the last time she felt this weary. Closing her eyes, snippets of memories filled her mind.

Coming here to pray for Mia. Camping with Gabby. Feeling lost and alone when her parents told her they were selling the ranch. Utter dejection when they sold it to Ryder.

She flung her forearm over her eyes. Why was she doing this to herself? What did she think was going to happen? Everything was just going to work out? That she'd get the guy, the twins and the family ranch? Life didn't work that way. Not for her. Life worked out for other women. The pretty, outgoing ones.

Eden sat up. She could hear her voice telling the girls, *Your beauty comes from who you are, not what you look like.*

When had she decided she was unattractive and defective?

She wasn't either. Sure, she was quiet, but that didn't make her ugly or incapable of being loved.

God, what is wrong with me? I've convinced myself that Ryder couldn't possibly love me, not after having been married to Lily. But why do I believe that?

A memory came back—one she'd forgotten—from long ago. It must have been early fall, Eden's freshman or sophomore year of high school. Mia had gotten a twinkle in her eye, grabbed Eden by the hand and said, "Come on, let's get out of here."

Mia had driven them to this very spot, where they'd joked around and talked about the future. It all came back to Eden as if it had happened yesterday.

"I'm not going to college." Mia had been firm. "I'm staying right here in Rendezvous. I mean, look at this." She'd expanded both arms out to the view before them. "Why would anyone leave?"

"What will you do?" Eden asked.

"Get married. Have a few kids."

Mia had a natural beauty and easy presence, and Eden didn't doubt it for a minute.

"I can't wait to see who you marry." Smiling, Mia nudged her.

"Me?"

"Yes, you." She laughed. "Who else would I be talking about? Whoever he is, he'll have to be pretty amazing to deserve you. Hey, do you think our husbands will be friends? Maybe we'll go on vacations together. Our kids will run around..."

The memory faded, and Eden was left with a sense of wonder.

Mia had firmly believed Eden would get married someday. There hadn't been a hint of hesitation. Mia had always thought the best of her.

And Eden had stopped believing in herself after Mia died.

What would her sister tell her in this situation? *Ryder's a great guy. I'll have to talk with him, of course, to make sure he understands how blessed he is to have you...but isn't it crazy? We'll be married to brothers!*

Something tickled Eden's hand, and she looked down at where an ant crawled over it. She shook the insect off.

I wish you were here, Mia. You'd tell me Lily doesn't hold a candle to me. You'd be wrong, of course, but you always gave me confidence. I lost it when you died. But I'm getting it back.

Eden tucked her knees to her chest and wrapped her arms around them as she took in the surrounding area. The beauty seeped into her bones, leaving her relaxed.

One of her favorite Bible passages came to mind, and she spoke it out loud. "He brought me forth also into a large place; He delivered me, because He delighted in me."

Lord, thank You for bringing me here, for letting me remember that day with Mia.

Maybe God always had more in mind for her.

Eden was ready to claim all His blessings. Starting now.

"Can we see Auntie Eden, Daddy?" Ivy asked from the back seat of his truck as they drove home from Mason's an hour later.

"Yeah, let's go see Auntie Eden!" Harper yelled.

"Uh, not right now, girls." He wanted nothing more than to drive to town and invade her apartment with the twins, but he didn't have that right.

Mason's comment about Eden being in the shadows kept jabbing his conscience.

She *was* in the shadows. She was humble. Kind. Loyal. Committed. Would do anything for her friends.

Everything he'd ever wanted in a woman.

"I miss her, Daddy. I *need* one of Auntie Eden's hugs," Ivy pleaded.

He knew the feeling. He needed her, too.

For so long he'd told himself—and everyone who'd listen—he was never falling in love again. Marriage wasn't for him. He'd thought he wasn't good at it, that he couldn't trust a woman to not break his heart.

But he'd been wrong. And he might not be able to prevent his heart from being broken, but he could tell Eden the truth—he loved her and wanted to make her happy.

What would make her happy?

He tapped the steering wheel with his thumbs. She never expected appreciation. She acted like being in the shadows was fine.

Well, it wasn't fine. He wanted her to know down to the last detail how much he appreciated her. He wanted to shout to the entire town that this woman was a priceless jewel.

Maybe he had something to offer that no one else had.

Pure love for her.

Devotion.

Commitment.

Lord, I need that woman. My girls do, too. How can I show her? How can I get through to her?

And it hit him.

"I've got an idea, girls." He glanced at them through the rearview mirror. "Why don't we throw a surprise party for Auntie Eden?"

They exchanged excited looks and squealed. "Yes!"

"I'll have to make some calls. I don't know if she's busy."

"I love parties!" Ivy clapped her hands.

"We need cake!" Harper kicked the seat in front of her.

He pulled into his drive, mentally listing everyone he needed to contact. Hopefully they'd be free. He'd ask Gabby to get Eden to his house. Nicole might be willing to contribute dessert. Mason could help grill burgers...

Ryder didn't have much time. He didn't want to wait a day, a week or a month. He was doing this now.

His lips curved into a grin.

And it just might work.

Chapter Fourteen

It was after six when Eden gave herself a final look-over in the mirror. She'd curled her hair, carefully applied her makeup and found a pretty short-sleeved blouse to wear with her favorite dark jeans. After driving home from her special place earlier, she'd stretched out on her bed and fallen into a deep sleep. When she'd woken, she'd been confused, then realized it was still Saturday, and she did indeed still need to take charge of her life.

She was going over to Ryder's.

Speaking of… She went into the kitchen where she'd left her phone earlier. She wanted to make sure he'd be home before driving there. She had so much to say.

Her phone showed three missed calls and two texts from Gabby. Hopefully, there wasn't an emergency. Her heartbeat thudded as she checked them.

Are you busy tonight? I need to talk.

Then Call or text me when you get this.

Weird. Gabby wasn't one to be dramatic. Something serious must have happened.

Eden called her. Gabby answered after the first ring. "Where have you been?"

"Napping. Why?" She closed her eyes tightly, silently praying that nothing bad had happened.

"Oh, good. I, uh, needed to talk to you. Are you busy tonight?"

"Kind of…" She should confide in Gabby, but she didn't know what to say.

"Can you cancel your plans?" Gabby sounded worked up.

"What's going on, Gabby? You're scaring me."

"I am? I'm sorry. I didn't mean to. I just need some advice."

"Okay."

"I'll pick you up. We can go out to dinner. It will give me an excuse to wear something besides yoga pants. I'll be there in five."

The line went dead. What had just happened? How had she gone from worrying about an emergency to going out to dinner with Gabby? In thirty seconds, no less?

She sighed. Her plans to talk to Ryder could wait until dinner was over. Maybe it would be better that way. If she got to his place later, the girls might be asleep, and she'd be able to talk to him privately.

Five minutes later, Gabby arrived looking bouncy and cheerful. This all felt very strange.

"Ooh, I love that shirt. You look really pretty, Eden."

"Thanks, so do you."

They walked to Gabby's car and got inside. As she drove, Gabby kept up a steady stream of commentary about the cute bathing suit she'd found online for Phoebe and the new bedspread she'd bought.

Gabby took a right at the stop sign, and Eden turned to her. "Hey, you went the wrong way."

"No, I didn't. We have to make a side trip first. Sorry."
She shrugged, then launched into how she and Dylan had
decided it was time to try for a baby.

"A baby? Really?" Eden perked up. "I hope you get
pregnant right away. Just think, Phoebe will have a little
brother or sister."

"I know, right?" Gabby's cheeks were flushed as she
smiled. "Will you pray for us?"

"Always."

As they chatted about babies, Eden's nerves got jittery.
Maybe after she talked to Ryder, he would still want to
date her. Maybe he'd even fall in love with her at some
point. And what if they got married? One day it would
be her turn to tell Gabby they were trying to have a baby.

Her palms grew clammy. So much depended on tonight's conversation. Maybe she should ask Gabby to turn
around. Or confide in her about her feelings for Ryder.
Ask her to take a rain check on dinner?

The countryside grew familiar. Why were they pull-
ing in to the ranch?

"Um, Gabby?"

"Yes?" Her innocent expression didn't fool Eden.

"Why are we at Ryder's?"

She drove up the driveway and parked. Then she
opened her door and waved for her to follow. "Come on."

"I'll wait out here." Eden stayed in the passenger seat.

"Look, I didn't want to say anything, but Mason called
me earlier and said the twins were upset this morning
when he and Brittany watched them. I'm dropping off
a little care package for them. But I think a word and a
hug from you would make a world of difference to them
right now."

If the girls were struggling…

She'd do her best to help them cope. Eden unbuckled

the seat belt and got out of the car. They walked to the front porch and knocked. The door opened, and they entered the house.

Something wasn't right. Where was Ryder? Who had opened the door? Why was it so quiet?

Gabby dragged her into the kitchen.

"Surprise!"

All of her friends were in there.

Had she forgotten a birthday or something?

Ryder strode forward and took Eden's hand. His eyes gleamed with affection for her. She couldn't look away and didn't want to. "Eden, welcome to your party."

"My party?" She loved the feel of her hand in his. Her heartbeat sped up. But she shook her head, even more confused than before. "What are you talking about?"

"It's our official Eden Page Appreciation Extravaganza."

Ivy, Harper and Noah raced over to her. "We're throwing you a party, Auntie Eden!"

Tears stung the backs of her eyes. "Why?"

Mason stepped forward. "Because you've done so much for us."

"You rescued us." Gabby slung her arm over Eden's shoulders and side-hugged her.

"You were there when we needed you the most." Nicole, holding Henry, stepped closer. Judd held Amelia, and Eden noticed Brittany carrying Eli.

Her knees wobbled. She couldn't take it all in. This party was for her?

"Come on." Ryder stayed close to her. "Let's take this to the family room." He leaned in and whispered, "You look beautiful."

Then he kept her hand in his as they all made their way to the back of the house. Everyone took seats, except the twins and Noah, who were playing in the corner with a cluster of balloons. The room had been decorated with crepe paper, balloons and a homemade sign that read We Love You, Eden.

She had to wipe away tears at the sight. She had no idea what this was all about, but she wanted to remember every second of it.

Ryder helped her sit on the couch, then moved to the center of the room, facing her. Everyone turned their attention to him.

"Eden, you've selflessly devoted yourself to each one of us, and we all want to pay you back in some small way." He gestured to Mason. "Do you want to begin?"

Mason grinned and stood. He gave Ryder a half embrace and took his spot.

"Eden, you were like a mother to Noah after Mia died. I don't know how you did it, considering you were grieving, too, but you're the main reason I was able to hang on that first year. I can never thank you enough or repay you for giving Noah such a firm foundation of love."

Noah ran up to her, and she hauled him onto her lap. He kissed her cheek and hugged her. "I love you!"

"I love you, too," Eden said, and then he hopped off her lap and ran back to the girls.

Gabby had switched spots with Mason. "Eden, you're my best friend. I don't know what I would have done without you after my sister died. Here I was, suddenly a single mom with no clue how to raise a baby or deal with my grief. But you stepped in and babysat Phoebe. You're the one who told me so many times that I was a great mom and that Allison would be proud. I love you, girl."

Nicole handed Henry to Mason and switched spots with Gabby.

"Last Christmas Eve, I was at one of the lowest points

in my life." Nicole's lips trembled. "And you showed up on my doorstep because I hadn't answered your texts and you didn't want me to spend Christmas Eve alone. I will *never* forget your kindness. You have no idea how much I needed you that night."

The lump forming in Eden's throat had grown to the size of a walnut. No matter how many times she swallowed, it wouldn't go away.

Ryder took Nicole's spot as she sat back down.

"I met you two Christmases ago, shortly after meeting my brother." Ryder nodded to Mason. "Eden, you weren't afraid to tell me the truth when you saw me behaving badly. Even then you had the twins' best interests in mind. I didn't like it—wasn't used to being called out. But it made a big impression on me."

She wasn't sure where he was going with this, but he looked so sincere and she couldn't look away.

"I was drawn to you. Am drawn to you. When I decided to move here, I knew one thing—you're the only one I was comfortable with watching my girls."

Ivy and Harper shouted, "We love you, Auntie Eden!"

She clapped her hand over her heart.

"You put your life on hold for us. You came here, to your childhood home, even though you had a lot of misgivings about it, and took care of not only Harper and Ivy but me, too. I am honored to call you my friend. I hope you know what a special person you are."

He crossed over to her then and held out his hand. She let him help her stand. He pulled her into his arms and hugged her. Then he whispered, "I have more to say to you, too, but not in front of the girls."

Everyone surrounded her, hugging her and telling her how much she meant to them.

"It's my turn." Eden waved them all to sit. "I don't

know what to say. This is more than I deserve. Mason, thank you for the privilege of taking care of Noah when he was a baby. It saved me from my grief over Mia."

He looked emotional himself as he nodded to her.

"Gabby, you *are* a terrific mother," Eden said. "You're my best friend. I would never have forgiven you if you wouldn't have let me babysit Phoebe. I love her. And I love you."

Gabby wiped under her eyes.

"Nicole," Eden said. "You're my hero. You took a desperate situation—losing your husband while pregnant with triplets—and chose to embrace your future. I know you and Judd are going to be very happy together."

Nicole smiled up at Judd, who'd placed his hand on her shoulder.

"And Ryder," Eden said. She couldn't tell him everything in front of the girls. It wouldn't be fair to them, but she owed him thanks, too. "I'm glad you moved here. You've given me the courage to want more from life."

Everyone stared at her, waiting in breathless anticipation. But she wanted to do this right. In private. Ivy and Harper had dealt with too many emotional ups and downs this week already.

"Thank you all." Eden's lips wobbled. "I don't know what I ever did to deserve such good friends."

"Let's get the cookout going," Mason hollered. As if on cue, everyone dispersed outside. Everyone except Ryder and the twins.

Ivy hugged her first. "I missed you."

"I missed you, too." Eden smoothed her hair away from her forehead. "And you, too, Harper."

Harper wrapped her arms around both her and Ivy.

"I'm sorry your mom couldn't stay longer." She kissed

both their cheeks. They nodded, their faces falling. "But I'm glad I got to meet her. She's very nice."

They glanced at each other and smiled. "She is nice."

"And I could tell she loved the gifts you made her."

"She took our books home with her." Harper's eyes shone.

"Mommy's getting married." Ivy's cheeks drooped.

"That's what I heard."

"We're flower girls." Harper shrugged.

"We get fancy dresses." Ivy didn't sound excited.

"Well, you'll be the prettiest girls there." Eden held the twins close. When she let them go, they smiled at her. "I love you both."

"Come on, Harper! Ivy!" Noah bellowed. "I'm gonna pop this balloon!"

The girls ran off.

And only Ryder remained.

Her heart was bursting with love for this man. She just prayed she had the right words to let him know exactly how important he was to her.

The twins ran outside and shut the sliding door so hard it bounced open an inch, but Ryder didn't care. He took Eden's hand in his and kissed the back of it.

"I can't believe you put all this together." She shook her head. "I was getting ready to text you to see if I could come over when Gabby called."

"You were going to come over?" Hope began to grow inside him.

Her eyes were shy as she nodded. "Yeah."

All he wanted to do was kiss her. Tell her how much she meant to him.

Tell her he loved her.

Her eyelashes dipped. "I wasn't entirely truthful with you this morning."

"Oh?" An uneasy pit formed in his stomach.

"I thought I was, but…" She met his eyes. "I *do* want to explore whatever this is between us. I felt inferior to Lily. It's not just her, though. You asked me if someone had broken my heart. The answer is no. I've never given it to anyone to break. Until now."

Was he hearing her correctly?

"I'm in love with you. I love you, Ryder. I didn't want to be, but I couldn't stop it." She stared at him through those rich brown eyes, and he was helpless to look away. "I've been attracted to you since we met. I lied that day when I said I wasn't. You're gorgeous. Smart. You get things done. You don't let anything get in your way. You love your daughters—I know you'd make any sacrifice for them."

A thousand things popped up to say to her, but none of them came out.

"As for exploring our feelings," she said, "I have to warn you, I'm kind of past the exploring phase. My heart is already yours."

He held his breath.

"But I think you should know…" She glanced down at her hands for a moment. "All I ever wanted was to get married, have a family and live on a ranch. Because of that, I don't want you to ever think I'm telling you I love you because of what you can offer me. I love you because you're a good man, a good father, a good friend."

He wrapped his hands around her back and hauled her to him. He could feel her heart beating against his chest. His was beating double-time.

"I love you, Eden." He stared down into her incredible eyes. "I love you. It feels so good to say it out loud. You're the most beautiful woman I've ever seen. And your heart—it's so big. I don't know how you do it. You give and give. I want to give *you* everything. I want to be worthy of you."

"You? Worthy of me?" She scrunched her nose and laughed. "You've got it all wrong."

"No, I don't." He wanted her to know he was dead serious. "I don't think there's a man on earth worthy of you. All the guys around here have thumbtacks for brains, and I'm glad. Because you're mine."

He leaned in and pressed his lips to hers. And she softened into his embrace. This woman. He'd never get his fill of her.

When he ended the kiss, she smiled. He tenderly brushed her lips with his thumb.

"Oh, my," she said.

His thoughts exactly.

"I think every day should be Eden Appreciation Day." He kept his hands on her waist, enjoying having her in his arms.

"My head would get too big."

"If it meant getting to hold you and kiss you, I wouldn't care."

"What will we tell the girls?"

"The truth," he said. "They can handle it."

"Are you sure? They've been through a lot."

"Yeah. But they deserve nothing less than the truth."

"I think you're right."

"Of course, I'm right." He grinned. "If, by chance, I'm wrong, I can always buy Harper a pony and promise Ivy a bunny."

"You're terrible." She chuckled, swatting at his chest.

"And you're wonderful. I'm your biggest fan, and I'll never stop letting everyone know how blessed I am to have you."

"You're the blessing, Ryder."

"I guess God blessed us both."

Epilogue

She was going to be their mommy! Eden hugged Ivy, then Harper. How blessed she was to nurture these children.

The twins were dressed in identical white dresses with tiaras in their curled hair, and each of them carried a small basket with rose petals. Organ music spilled from the church to where they stood near the entrance to the sanctuary.

"Are you ready, girls?" Eden fluffed the material of her wedding gown and tried to rein in her nerves.

"Yes!" they said in unison.

"You look bee-yoo-tiful." Ivy had stars in her eyes.

"You look like Cinderella." Harper nudged Noah, in his tuxedo. "Doesn't she look like Cinderella?"

"You do, Auntie Eden. You're even prettier than Cinderella." He clutched a white satin pillow with the wedding rings on top. "I'd marry you if Uncle Ryder didn't."

"Thank you, Noah-bear." Her heart was overflowing with love. "All three of you are making our day very special."

"It's time." One of the church ladies pointed to the children. Noah pulled back his shoulders and walked between the girls as they tossed rose petals down the aisle of the church. Eden spotted Gabby, her matron of honor, at the front standing next to Nicole and Brittany in their pretty coral dresses. Dylan and Judd were across the aisle with Mason, who was Ryder's best man.

Eden hadn't seen Ryder yet, and she edged closer to her dad. Her knees felt wobbly, and her heart was ready to beat out of her chest. She'd already cried twice that morning, and the self-manicure incident had thrown her into a panic. Maybe if she kept her hands tucked under the bouquet, no one would notice the clumps of glitter in the polish.

"You ready, honey?" Dad took her hand and rested it on his arm. "You look beautiful. I couldn't be happier for you. You've got a good man, there."

"Thanks, Dad." A memory of Mia and Dad at this very spot years ago brought a sense of calm to her nerves.

Life was full of ups and downs, and she was ready for them. She'd started her online classes a few weeks ago, and now she'd have a partner to weather whatever came her way.

They waited another moment and then headed down the aisle.

And there was Ryder.

She locked eyes with him and held her breath. He looked like a model in his tux, but it was the intensity in his eyes that sent a thrill down her spine. Like in a dream, she was vaguely aware of Dad leaving her with Ryder, and she barely heard the pastor's words as he conducted the service.

Before she knew it, she and Ryder had exchanged vows and the ring was on her finger. Then the announcement came—they were man and wife. It was really true!

They made their way to the back of the church and out

onto the lawn where the guests would greet them. The late-September sun made everything shiny and special.

"Mrs. Fanning." Ryder swept her into his arms and twirled her around. "You look—wow—you take my breath away."

She smiled, reaching up to give him a light kiss. "You look handsome, more than handsome."

"But you…wow, you are magnificent." He kissed her with passion. His kiss promised everything she'd ever wanted, and she sank into his embrace.

A round of applause interrupted them, and she looked up at him, her face on fire as he ended the kiss, keeping his arm around her waist.

All their family and friends surrounded them, offering well wishes and congratulations. Eden took it all in and said a silent prayer of thanks. Nicole and Judd were holding hands––they'd gotten married a month ago in a small ceremony. Gabby had the slightest baby bump under her gown as she gestured for Dylan to hand her Phoebe. Mason and Brittany had announced last night at the rehearsal dinner they were expecting a baby, too. And Ryder had whispered that he wanted a baby ASAP. At which she told him he needed to make an honest woman of her first. He'd responded with "Twenty-four hours."

The next hour was a blur of hugs and well wishes and pictures.

"Well, my lovely bride," he said as the bridal party dispersed. "How are you holding up?"

"Fabulous."

"Mama!" Ivy and Harper ran to her and threw their arms around her waist.

Eden was shocked. Ryder merely smiled and tilted his head. "I told them they could call you whatever they wanted."

"Are you sure you want to call me that?" She hugged the girls. "You don't have to, you know."

"We want to." Harper slung her arm over Ivy's shoulders. "Right, Ivy?"

"Right." She nodded, her eyes twinkling. "Mommy's far away, but Mama lives with us."

Eden's heart spilled over. She pulled them close to her. "I love you so much. I'm honored."

"We love you, too."

"You're everything I've ever wanted, Eden." He tucked her arm in his. "I plan on showing you my appreciation every day."

"Every day, huh?" She pressed her palm against his chest and stared up at him.

"Yes." His eyes smoldered. "What do you want? Name it. It's yours."

"You've already given me everything, Ryder. All I want is you."

* * * * *

*Don't miss the previous books in Jill Kemerer's
Wyoming Sweethearts miniseries!*

Her Cowboy Till Christmas
The Cowboy's Secret
The Cowboy's Christmas Blessing

Available now from Love Inspired Books!

Dear Reader,

It's hard to believe this series has come to an end. I've enjoyed these characters so much. If you've read the first three books, you'll know how much energy and love Eden invests into her friends. I knew she had to have a man who would celebrate all her amazing qualities. Ryder is that man and more. He needed a support group as much as Mason, Eden, Gabby and Nicole did, and he found a lifelong friendship with them. I can imagine him and Eden raising the girls in Rendezvous. Harper, naturally, will be competing in rodeos with Noah, and Ivy will take dance lessons at Brittany's studio and babysit the triplets as soon as she's old enough.

Like Eden, I think we all have times when we feel invisible or unappreciated. Please don't get discouraged if you're in one of those times. God sees everything you're doing, and He's smiling on your efforts even if they're unnoticed by others. He delights in you!

Thank you for reading my books. Your support means more to me than you'll ever know. I love connecting with readers. Feel free to email me at jill@jillkemerer.com or write me at PO Box 2802, Whitehouse, Ohio, 43571.

God bless you,
Jill Kemerer

WE HOPE YOU ENJOYED
THIS BOOK FROM

LOVE INSPIRED
INSPIRATIONAL ROMANCE

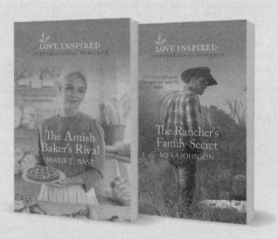

Uplifting stories of faith, forgiveness and hope.

Fall in love with stories where faith helps
guide you through life's challenges, and discover
the promise of a new beginning.

6 NEW BOOKS AVAILABLE EVERY MONTH!

SPECIAL EXCERPT FROM

LOVE INSPIRED
INSPIRATIONAL ROMANCE

*When a young Amish woman returns home
with a baby in tow, will sparks fly with her
handsome—and unusual—neighbor?*

Read on for a sneak preview of
The Baby Next Door
by Vannetta Chapman.

Grace found Nicole had pulled herself up to the front door
and was high-fiving none other than Adrian Schrock.
He'd squatted down to her level. Nicole was having a fine
old time.

Grace picked up her *doschder* and pushed open the
door, causing Adrian to jump up, then step back toward
the porch steps. It was, indeed, a fine spring day. The sun
shone brightly across the Indiana fields. Flowers colored
yellow, red, lavender and orange had begun popping
through the soil that surrounded the porch. Birds were
even chirping merrily.

Somehow, all those things did little to elevate Grace's
mood. Neither did the sight of her neighbor.

Adrian resettled his straw hat on his head and smiled.
"Gudemariye."

"Your llama has escaped again."

"Kendrick? *Ya.* I've come to fetch him. He seems to
like your place more than mine."

"I don't want that animal over here, Adrian. He spits.
And your peacock was here at daybreak, crying like a
child."

Adrian laughed. "When you moved back home, I guess you didn't expect to live next to a Plain & Simple Exotic Animal Farm."

Adrian wiggled his eyebrows at Nicole when he seemed to realize that Grace wasn't amused.

"I think of your place as Adrian's Zoo."

"Not a bad name, but it doesn't highlight our Amish heritage enough."

"The point is that I feel like we're living next door to a menagerie of animals."

"Up, Aden. Up."

Adrian scooped Nicole from Grace's hold, held her high above his head, then nuzzled her neck. Adrian was comfortable with everyone and everything.

"Do you think she'll ever learn to say my name right?"

"Possibly. Can you please catch Kendrick and take him back to your place?"

"Of course. That's why I came over. I guess I must have left the gate open again." He kissed Nicole's cheek, then popped her back into Grace's arms. "You should bring her over to see the turtles."

As he walked away, Grace wondered for the hundredth time why he wasn't married. It was true that he'd picked a strange profession. What other Amish man raised exotic animals? No, Adrian wouldn't be considered excellent marrying material by most young Amish women.

Don't miss
The Baby Next Door *by Vannetta Chapman,*
available April 2021 wherever
Love Inspired books and ebooks are sold.

LoveInspired.com